❖ ❖ ❖

Her heart pounding, Misty abruptly rose, knocking her chair over and throwing Gene off balance. He and his chair toppled to the floor.

Misty released a squeal of horror and dropped to her knees. Gene lay still, his strong masculine body suddenly appearing frail and vulnerable. Could he have injured his head in the fall she wondered, panic rising. Remembering her CPR training, she gently shook his shoulders and shouted, "Are you all right?"

A strong arm snaked around her waist and pulled her down on top of him. Air left her lungs in a gust of, "Oh! Let me go!"

Her protest was useless. Effectively pinned against his hard body, her heart beat wildly, every nerve at attention. She lay stiff and still as porcelain, absorbing his masculine scent. He capped the back of her head in one large hand, coaxing her lips to his. She closed her eyes as his full, sensuous lips caressed her waiting mouth. Then it was over. Grinning, he released her.

Damn his beautiful hide! He knows I wanted him to kiss me. He's toying with me. Well, I'm not a Barbie Doll to be played with.

Instead of jumping off him as he obviously expected, she combed her fingers into his hair and brought her lips down hard against his, kissing him deeply. Smiling, she rolled off him and leapt to her feet.

Gene struggled to a sitting position, then to his feet. He watched Misty hustle out the door. Well, that bit of horseplay backfired, he thought. *Damn, she's good.*

❖ ❖ ❖

DINNER FOR TWO

ARLENE EVANS

Echelon Press Publishing
9735 Country Meadows Lane 1-D
Laurel, MD 20723
www.echelonpress.com

Copyright © 2005 by Arlene Evans
ISBN: 1-59080-436-8
Library of Congress Control Number: 2005936792

First Echelon Press paperback printing: January 2006
10 9 8 7 6 5 4 3 2 1

Cover Artist: © Nathalie Moore
2004 Arianna Best in Category Winner

Printed in the USA

Dedication

To my family who have provided much love and encouragement along the way.

Acknowledgements

The assistance of Russell S. Worrall, OD, Professor of Optometry, U.C. Berkeley, has been invaluable.

"It is not true that we have only one life to live; if we can read, we can live as many more lives and as many kinds of lives as we wish."

S.I. Hayakawa

Chapter 1

The cold steel molded to Gene Haynes' hand like a snug leather glove. Reverently, he squeezed the trigger. His hand spasmed as the slug exploded from the barrel. Sizzling in on target, the gray missile entered, then erupted from the victim's bald head. Crimson sprayed against white walls. The body lay lifeless on the drawing room floor. Gene smiled. This scene was his finest creation to date.

"Oh, Mr. Haynes," Mrs. Anderson gushed, fanning her eyelashes and smiling crookedly to create dimples in her ample cheeks. "You're so creative! My guests will love your cake! It's simply perfect for my murder-mystery dinner."

Pastry tube in hand, Gene nodded his agreement. He prided himself on decorating his cakes to personalize an event or individual. He'd question the customer until he discovered something unusual about the occasion or unique about the person the cake was being ordered for. In short, he got involved with his cakes. They weren't just to eat. They were to experience.

He had never experienced one of his creations more fully than this one. Frankly, a murder scene was more interesting than dabbing on rings of pink rosebuds. Rosebuds were intrinsic to cake decorating, however, so he tolerated them. He was good at intricate decorations, too, in spite of massive fingers that were out of place doing such delicate work, and in spite of the fact that he couldn't tell one color from another. Except blue and yellow, which he used as extensively as he could.

His color vision problem was another reason Gene enjoyed doing the murder scene on this particular cake. Except for the crimson "blood," which he had identified by the label on the tube of icing, it was in black and white, easy for him to discern.

Carefully, he placed his rectangular piece of art in an appropriate box, tied it with string, and turned it over to Mrs. Anderson.

"Can I get you anything else for your party?"

She scanned the deli's refrigerator display case. "Well...not for the party, but I'll have half a pound of the dilled potato salad for dinner."

"Excellent choice." Gene scooped the salad into a container, weighed it, and passed it to her. "Have a great evening."

"Thank you so much," she squealed. Her squat legs revved up for action and she scuttled out the door.

The phone rang.

"*Dinner for Two*," he answered.

"Ms. Haynes, please."

The sultry, Lauren Bacall-if-you-want-anything-just-whistle-sounding voice piqued his interest.

"This is Gene Haynes."

Flustered, the feminine voice blurted, "Oh, I'm sorry. I thought it was 'Jean,' I mean, I expected a woman."

This wasn't the first time a caller had assumed he'd be female. He'd fought his way through grammar school over being called "Jeannie-Weenie." But by seventh grade he was the biggest kid in school, and his ruddy complexion and burnished hair gave him a mean, tough look enhanced by glowering that he practiced daily in front of his bedroom mirror. It was worth it. All the teasing–and the fighting–stopped.

He noted, however, anxiety in the sexy, warm voice, and assumed it was not over his being a man.

"It's okay. It happens," he said, trying to soothe her. "What can I do for you?"

"I'd like a dinner for two…in my apartment."

How about you and me, he thought, imagining a face and form to compliment the perfection of the voice.

"You called the right place." In doing market research, Gene had discovered that no other catering service in Sacramento would do dinners for fewer than six. He had decided to fill that void, and at the same time supplement his income while building up a steady clientele in his newly opened gourmet delicatessen and bakery.

In the process, he discovered he enjoyed doing the dinners for two. He not only took food to the customer's home, but also the table, chairs, and everything else needed for the dinner, including music of the client's choice. He'd cook a gourmet dinner, serve it, then quietly and efficiently pack up everything and leave. The couple was generally in a romantic mood by that time and didn't want him hanging around.

"Did you have a theme in mind?" he asked.

The voice hesitated. "No, not really. What kinds of dinners do you do?"

"You name it. French is popular. Japanese, Chinese, Italian, Scandinavian–"

"How about straight American?" she interjected.

So she'll be entertaining a meat and potato man, he thought. Too bad. She sounded more interesting than that. "Prime rib?"

"Good. And twice-stuffed potatoes?"

"Can do."

She sighed audibly. "I'll leave the rest up to your judgment."

She doesn't want to be bothered, he mused. He wondered why. Usually, women fussed unceasingly over all the minor details. "You'd like the evening to have a romantic atmosphere?" he said, more as a statement than a question. Every dinner he'd done had been romantic.

"Uh, well…no."

His mouth curled in a knowing grin. In other words, she wants to interest the guy but she doesn't want to get too friendly with him.

"No candles?"

"No, no candles."

She sounded irritated with the question

"Wine?"

"One bottle. Whatever will go well with the beef."

"Good." He liked making the decisions about the wine. "And music?"

"I don't care about the music. Bring whatever you'd like to hear." She sounded impatient, like she wanted the interview to be over. Maybe she's in a quandary and doesn't know exactly what she wants to happen as a result of this dinner, he thought.

"One other question before we get to the details of time and place. Colors."

"Colors?"

"You wouldn't want the table setting to clash with your decor."

"Oh, I see. No, of course not." Her voice trailed off. "Um, the living room–where we'll be eating–is done in muted browns and peach with accents of green."

Swell. Green and brown. They both looked the same to him. "Okay. I'll keep that in mind." He shifted the receiver to his left ear, scrunching his shoulder to his jaw to hold it in place. He picked up a pen. "Your name?"

"Misty Jones."

Misty. That complimented her voice. He thought of a low, misty, rolling, enveloping tulle fog.

"Address and telephone number?" He recorded the information as she recited it. "Now when did you want this dinner?"

"Do you have Saturday evening the eighteenth open?"

Gene checked his calendar. "Nope. Sorry. How about Sunday the nineteenth?"

"*Hmm*...yes. That would be all right."

"Good. I'll keep in touch." He hung up, then glanced around his deli. Eight gleaming alabaster tables for four and two for two. He longed for the day they'd be full. He was certain he was in a good location, near California's State Capitol building. As soon as the legislators discovered him, he'd have more business than he could handle.

The back door opened to admit a gust of wind and, belly first, Sam Bronstone, Gene's part-time help. Gene regarded the large paunchy thirty-five year old with disdain. Eyes narrow, he said, "If you're late one more time, you're outta here."

Sam waved his arm as if brushing away the complaint. "Cool it. I haven't noticed big crowds pouring in for lunch. And for what you pay me, you're lucky I'm here at all."

Unfortunately, Gene knew Sam was right. He also knew Sam milked the customers with his gift of gab for more tips than he was worth. A real salesman. And with his gargantuan appetite, Sam made sure there were no excess profits.

"I was at driving school," Sam explained. "Truck driving school. I'll be making big bucks in a real man's job before you know it."

So there it was again. Gene wasn't a real man's name. And operating a deli and catering service wasn't a real man's job. If he didn't need the help, he'd see to it that the rotund toad had an assisted hop straight out the door.

"Cut the banter and get to work."

Mumbling to himself, Sam covered his Levis and plaid shirt with a starched white apron.

Misty straightened from a crouched position, placed her hands on the small of her back, then arched to relieve her muscle tension. Her senses were drawn to the soothing sounds and gentle movements of the Sacramento River. The glistening water lazily streamed down, pirouetting along its course. A family of four on a Huck Finn-styled raft leisurely drifted with the mellow, dancing current.

"*Psst*, Misty!" Lorna Blake elbowed her friend in the ribs. "Get a load of the hunk up there!" She nodded toward the top of the riverbank.

"I thought you came along to help me find accents for my displays, not to look at 'hunks,'" Misty complained. She brushed straight, wispy bangs away from her eyes.

"Well, we could do both, couldn't we?" asked Lorna.

Misty glanced at her roommate, a petite twenty-five year old whose hair was as blond as Misty's was dark. She let her eyes follow Lorna's gaze and was momentarily taken aback by the godly-looking creature on the crest of the bank, standing, feet apart, hands on hips, appearing to be surveying his creation. Black shorts covered massive legs to mid-thigh. Below the shorts, fine, tightly curled russet hair clothed his legs, matching the longer, thicker hair that crowned his rugged, angular features. He wore jogging shoes and a white tee shirt.

Wide-eyed, Misty swallowed. Forcing her gaze away

from the regal presence, she again looked at her roommate. Lorna stood, feet apart, hands on hips. "What are you doing?" Misty demanded.

Lorna straightened before answering. "I've heard that successful flirting involves mirroring movements." She touched her right ear. Misty glanced up to see the sun god touching his left ear. She flushed in vexation and embarrassment for her roommate who, at that moment, dropped her left arm to her side. Without looking, she knew the "hunk" had dropped his right arm.

"For heaven sakes, cut it out!" Misty ordered.

"But this really works," Lorna protested. "I've read all about it. He won't be able to resist me." Lorna rotated her body, turning her profile to the object of her desire.

Reluctantly admitting to herself that she wanted to view the apparition again, Misty rolled her eyes heavenward to see the russet head turn. The muscular body jogged out of sight.

Relief and disappointment co-mingled. Then Misty reminded herself of other absurdly appealing men she had known. She had gone steady with an Adonis in high school until she discovered that he wasn't going steady with her. She dated another gorgeous man in college, but grew weary of other girls' longing, lustful, liquid gazes. What was more disconcerting was the way he had bathed in their adoration. Neither of those self-centered men believed it was decent or honorable to limit their favors to one woman. Yes...she had had quite enough of beautiful men.

"Good. He's gone," Misty said. "Now you can get

back to work."

"Slave driver," Lorna mumbled. She poked through river rocks looking for small smooth stones. Her favorites had touches of muted colors on their gray backgrounds.

Delighted to find several pieces of gnarled driftwood, Misty's mind raced ahead to arrangements she would create with them. Her thoughts were interrupted when Lorna whined, "Let's stop for lunch."

"Okay," Misty agreed. "I think we've found enough intriguing rocks and wood to keep me busy for some time."

They removed their backpacks, then unzipped them to unload crackers, cheese, fruit and soft drinks. They used the nylon bags to sit on while they ate.

A bevy of teenagers, bellowing out favorite songs, drifted by on an inflated rubber raft. Misty smiled, recalling similar excursions in her high school days. "I've never seen the Mississippi," she said, "but it couldn't be more beautiful than this."

Lorna popped the top of a cola can. "What if Raymond won't loan you the money?"

Misty inhaled sharply. "He has to. I need that Victorian home. It's perfect for my floral business." She paused. "And the living quarters upstairs are ideal for you and me."

Skeptically, Lorna nodded. "Uh, sure. I'd like to live there. But just in case the loan doesn't work out, what's 'Plan B?'"

Misty regarded an apple dejectedly. Her friend was

usually the flighty one, the one whose plan was not to plan, but to let tomorrow take care of itself. Now, however, Misty was forced to admit she didn't have a 'Plan B.' She squeezed her apple until her thumb broke through the red skin, squirting out juice on the crackers.

Lorna flinched. "Watch it."

Misty stared at the well her thumb had made in the apple. "This just has to work out. It would be my dream come true. Raymond can't pass up a bargain and the house is on the market at a bargain price."

"But do you think it's a good idea to try to snag him at your cozy dinner tonight?"

Misty frowned. "I have no desire to 'snag' him. We have no romantic interest in each other."

Lorna shrugged. "Why don't you just call him on the telephone to talk about it?"

"That's not the way business is done. More deals are finalized over meals than in board rooms."

"Then why not take him out to dinner?" Lorna persisted.

"We've been out to eat twice, and both times he was surrounded by people, both men and women, wanting to curry favors from him. I need to speak with him alone."

"Well, I wouldn't want to be alone with Raymond. He's a spoiled rich kid and has a weird glint in his eye."

"Don't be silly. He's an old family friend. I've known him since I was a child. I've nothing to fear from Raymond."

Lorna steepled her right brow. "Maybe so."

Gene parked his van at the curb, filled his arms with the first load of food and equipment, then walked up to the apartment building.   He scanned the nameplates, located *Jones,* and punched the bell with a bent elbow. When the door opened, his jaw slackened.   Standing before him was the girl, or rather, grown woman, he had dallied to watch that morning at the river. She had looked like a girl, though, as she poked through the rocks, picking up bits of this and that and lovingly placing them in a plastic sack. A tee shirt had been tucked into blue jeans that hugged her gently rounded hips and slim waist.

He had watched with pleasure while she brushed ebony bangs away from her obsidian eyes.   When she stood to stretch her aching back, he considered jogging down and offering to massage the kinks out. He grinned inwardly, thinking he had never tried that particular approach. But he had had a lot to accomplish that day and needed to get back to the deli, so decided to forego the pleasure. I'll search for her again another time, he had thought.

Now here she was before him, no longer an imaginary vision, but a very real flesh and blood female whose face and form perfectly matched her sensual voice. She was dressed in a black business suit and white blouse. Black hose clung to curvaceous calves and alluring ankles. Her gleaming hair was brushed into a bun and fastened at the nape of her lean, tapered, alabaster neck. She wore only a hint of makeup. Very nice, but what was with her anyway?   She looked like she was power dressed, heading out for a job interview instead of entertaining a man in her apartment. Women who ordered his dinners were usually dressed, if not in diaphanous gowns, at least in feminine evening clothes.

Misty realized she was staring. The bronzed apparition from the river had materialized on her doorstep. In spite of the fact that he wasn't standing on a pedestal surveying his domain, he still looked every inch a reigning deity. He wore dark tailored pants that molded to his masculine thighs. A black tee shirt peeked out from under the neckline V of his white chef's coat.

"Mr. Haynes?" She blinked, trying to avert her gaze from the harmony of blue and gold that pooled his eyes into a liquid emerald green.

"Gene," he amended.

Noting the tiny freckles sprinkled symmetrically across his perfect features, she stepped back, widening the door. "Uh...come in."

Recovered from his initial shock at seeing the woman he had so recently fantasized about, he mumbled, "The kitchen?"

With a raised hand she indicated the direction. He followed her pointed fingers and unloaded his supplies on the kitchen table.

"I'll get the other stuff and be right back." When he returned, he carried a small round table into the living room and placed it in front of her white brick fireplace. "Okay here?"

She nodded. "That's fine." She knew her voice sounded impatient, but she was annoyed that her heart had picked up speed from just watching this large man maneuver around her tiny apartment.

He glanced about the room, getting an impression of feminine coziness. "I think I should start a fire," he said.

"No, that won't be necessary." Silently, she chastised herself for sounding rude. After all, it wasn't his fault he was so ruggedly handsome.

Probably sounds too romantic to her, he thought. But fires had always seemed masculine to him, and this room needed a touch of manliness.

"The food will taste better," he persisted.

She sighed in resignation. "Very well, if you wish." She watched while he deftly arranged paper, kindling and then logs.

When the fire caught, Gene turned his attention to the table. First, he covered it, removing the tag that stated *peach* from the cloth. He smoothed the cloth with his hands. Next he arranged off-white china edged in gold. A matching gold rim circled the tops of the wine glasses.

Satisfied with the table setting, he examined the room more closely. A patterned couch faced the fireplace, with a contrasting easy chair and ottoman skewed to the side. An abundance of shelves decorated the walls, vehicles to display assortments of dried floral and driftwood arrangements.

"You did these?" he asked.

She tensed, hoping he liked them, yet upset that she cared at all about his opinion. "Yes."

He nodded approvingly. "Very nice." Then he realized he was gazing, not at her floral arrangements, but rather at the distribution of her physical attributes.

She squirmed uncomfortably. "Thank you."

"So that's what you were doing at the river this morning. Collecting driftwood."

"Oh–did you see us there?" Her cheeks heated, recalling Lorna's behavior and her own initial, wide-eyed reaction to his startling appearance. She blinked against her widening eyes, forcing her eyelids to a more neutral position.

She saw me there, he thought. Her blonde friend was doing her best to attract my attention. "Yeah. It was a great day to be by the river." They stood in silence a few moments, gazes mingled, then he added, "I'll set up the CD and get busy in the kitchen." He surveyed the room's lighting. "Don't you want some of these lights off–at least muted?"

"No!"

Puzzled, but vaguely pleased that she wasn't interested in romance with her dinner partner, he shrugged and went to the CD player. The motivation for this dinner was a mystery to him, just like the lovely lady who had ordered it. But he liked mysteries. And this one just might be a pleasure to solve.

Misty disappeared into her bedroom. Watching Gene was too unnerving. She picked up the script she had written for her evening's performance, ran through it, then stood in front of the mirror and tried to practice her lines. But an image of massive, muscular hands preparing the dinner she was to eat that evening appeared in the mirror. She blinked and swallowed hard, again concentrating on her lines. The doorbell chimed.

Tense, she took a deep, steadying breath, told herself to relax, and emerged from her bedroom to answer the door. She heard movements in the kitchen as she walked past and smelled what would ordinarily be delicious aromas; however, tension precluded hunger, so the wafting scents didn't appeal to her.

Her body winced when the bell rang again. She opened the door to Raymond Lane whom she had known since kindergarten. They had been neighbors, walked to school together, and played together. Their parents socialized. That is, until the Lanes inherited several million dollars from a despised relative who instantly transformed into a favored uncle and built a stately mansion in the best part of town, after which the two families rarely saw each other.

At five feet ten inches, Raymond stood two inches taller than Misty. He had a full brown mustache, a hint of sideburns, and a receding hairline. He prided himself on keeping physically fit, and his expensive slacks and shirt were tailored to suggestively strain against his body. He smiled, displaying the end result of expensive, extensive orthodontia treatment.

"Now that you've invited me over here, are you going to invite me in?"

Misty forced a return smile, then realized she still held her script in her left hand. She crumpled it. "Yes, of course." She escorted him to the living room, then, grateful for the fire, dropped her paper into the flames.

Raymond shrugged off his Armani jacket and draped it on the couch.

"How are your parents?" Misty inquired.

"Still rich," he responded, grinning at his quip. As an afterthought he asked, "And yours?"

"They're fine, thanks. Enjoying their retirement in Arizona. Please make yourself comfortable."

He flopped on the couch with a "Whew!"

Misty edged to the other side of the couch and sat sideways, leaving a cushion between them. "Hard day?"

"Exhausting. Eighteen holes of golf this morning. Lunch at the club. You know. Busy, busy."

She smiled, attempting to look interested in his little speech.

Gene appeared carrying an ornately carved silver tray with artistically arranged appetizers.

Raymond straightened, regarding the presence before him. "You hired this guy?"

Gene grimaced.

"Yes. I wanted to be able to relax and not fuss with dinner. Like eating out in."

"Good idea." He plucked a lettuce leaf spread with liver pate, looked at it suspiciously, sniffed it, then deigned to take a bite. "Where'd you find him?"

Gene's scowling brows melded into one.

"His service was recommended by a friend and I thought a dinner for two in my apartment would give us the perfect chance to visit."

Raymond raised his arm to rest it on top of the couch. "Yes. The evening does have possibilities."

Gene frowned at the leer on Raymond's face, then turned to Misty. "Would you like wine now or with dinner?"

"Both," Raymond answered, without looking at Gene. He licked his fingertips.

Gene retreated to the kitchen to return with the uncorked wine that had been resting. He poured and served the wine.

Raymond raised his glass to the light, squinting to peer through the wine. He swirled it, sniffed it, then sipped. "Not bad."

Not Bad! Gene gritted his teeth. This was *Clos Pegase*, an award-winning Cabernet Sauvignon. He had chosen it because its delicate spice character was accentuated with exactly the correct amount of oak to compliment the meat dish. He stared at Raymond whose second swallow of the wine was a large gulp. This scumbag wouldn't know a good wine if I clobbered him with it, Gene thought. Which doesn't sound like a bad idea. He went to the stereo and slipped in a CD of Mozart.

"I hate Mozart," Raymond complained. "Mother forced me to take piano lessons and this piece was the teacher's favorite."

Not after you got through mangling it, Gene silently mused. What does a girl like Misty see in a bum like him? Surely she isn't a fortune hunter, just after the guy's money. She didn't seem like that kind of girl. On the other hand, he really didn't know her, but for some reason he couldn't explain, he didn't want to think badly of her.

"It seems that every time we're together people surround you," Misty said.

Gene shook his head in bewilderment. That sounded like a come-on. He retreated to the kitchen.

Raymond scooted closer to her. "Yes, that must be difficult for you, but that's the way with the wealthy, I'm afraid. Inundated by people who want favors."

A shard of guilt pierced Misty. She decided to wait until the main course to bring up the subject of the loan.

Mistaking her look of guilt for one of longing, Raymond said, "Don't be sad, Misty dear. I'm all yours tonight. Actually, until you invited me here tonight, I never suspected you had anything but sisterly feelings for me. But then, we're not children any longer, are we?" He moved toward her until his left hand rested on her shoulder.

Misty swooped up the tray of hors d'oeuvres, effectively blocking Raymond's creeping right hand that was heading directly toward her knee. "Try one of these *Rumakis*. They're delicious."

While gazing at Misty, Raymond plucked one and popped it into his mouth. "Damn!" came a muffled mumble. "These things have toothpicks." He fished the piece of wood from his mouth and dropped it on the coffee table.

Gene re-entered the living room carrying a tray with two bowls of steaming soup. He noted Misty scrunched in the corner of the couch appearing to distance herself from Raymond's touch. She doesn't *look* like she's baiting him, he thought, perplexed. He arranged the soup bowls on the table.

"Soup is served," he announced.

Misty and Raymond took their places at the table. Sounds of the Glen Miller band wafted to their ears.

Raymond wrinkled his brow. "What is this guy—a throwback to the forties?"

Biting his inner cheek, Gene turned so the pair wouldn't observe his menacing glower.

"I've always enjoyed the sounds of the big bands," Misty said. She took a sip of soup. "Umm...the soup is wonderful."

Gene's facial muscles softened. She has good taste in music and food, he thought, but apparently not in men.

Raymond stared suspiciously into his soup bowl. "Looks like broccoli."

"Yes. It's the most delicious broccoli soup I've ever tasted." Misty tried to look enthusiastic as she brought another spoonful to her lips. It was superb soup, but the evening wasn't going as she had planned. Raymond's behavior was definitely out of character, and the handsome chef was more than distracting. Her usual hearty appetite had been replaced by nagging nausea.

"Can't abide broccoli. Gassy." Raymond raised his wine glass. "More wine."

"Yes, sir." Gene grasped the bottle, resisting the urge to pour it on Raymond's thinning hair. He refilled the pair's glasses, then went to the kitchen to prepare the next course. Why the hell should he care who she chooses to date he asked himself. She was nothing to him. Yet his gut contracted with the thought of having to face the pair again.

He stared at the few ounces of wine left in the bottle.

Battling with his own impulses, he raised the bottle to his lips and took a hearty swig. *Good lord, what a way to treat a fine wine!* He set the bottle down with a thud, his insides warmed, but not soothed.

Squaring his shoulders, Gene marched back to the living room to serve French bread and butter along with the salad, a mixture of delicate greens with a light vinegar and oil dressing.

Raymond munched on his salad and ate several pieces of bread.

Misty directed his gaze to her wall arrangements. "As you can see, I've been very busy in my business."

"Ah, yes. You always were clever. I fancy them, actually, although Mother would call them dust catchers."

Misty's stomach rolled.

Gene's eyes blazed.

"They're popular as accent pieces," she said.

"But one can hardly make a living doing that."

She nibbled a piece of French bread and chewed thoughtfully. "No, of course not. One must diversify. I just finished a big job for a group of model homes. Massive dried flower arrangements." She hesitated. "I really need a shop where I can offer a full range of floral services."

So what she wants is to talk business. The puzzle pieces fell into place. *No wonder she didn't want a romantic dinner theme. And that's the reason she's power dressed.* Feeling an inexplicable relief, Gene removed the salad plates and went to the kitchen

When he returned with the main course, Raymond

was drumming on the table with his fork. Gene served the prime rib, potatoes, and vegetables.

"Now this more like it," Raymond said. "Real food."

Gene nodded with comprehension. He understood why Misty had ordered prime rib.

Misty picked at her meal while Raymond wolfed his.

Mustering her courage, Misty said, "I wanted to discuss a business arrangement with you, Raymond."

He frowned, then winked. "Really? I have a little business in mind, too."

Gene escaped to the kitchen before he succumbed to the urge to apply the business end of his fist to Raymond's square jaw. But he remained close enough to the doorway to hear their conversation.

"*Ahh...*" Misty started. "I have my eye on a lovely Victorian home. It's zoned commercial and in a perfect location for a business. It has living quarters upstairs."

"Sounds convenient," Raymond said, a sly grin creeping across his face.

Misty cleared her throat. "It's been a women's clothing boutique, and the owner had so much business she had to move to larger quarters."

Raymond licked his thumb. "Is that so?"

"Yes. And if you saw it, I'm sure you'd agree it's on the market at a bargain price."

"More wine," Raymond demanded, raising his glass.

"Right away," Gene responded from the kitchen. Misty had ordered only one bottle of wine, which now depleted, so he rummaged around in the kitchen until he found a partially empty bottle of jug wine. He unscrewed the top and poured several ounces in the expensive bottle. He served it and watched as Raymond took a generous swallow. As Gene had guessed, the jerk couldn't tell the difference.

Raymond reached across the table and captured Misty's hand. "I'm glad you asked me here tonight. I never realized how I've yearned to be alone with you, too."

You've known her for years and only now want to be alone with her? Incredible.

Eyes downcast, Misty eased her hand out from under his. "You know I've always treasured your friendship, Raymond. I thought this evening would be an ideal time to talk business."

That's the way to handle him, Gene silently encouraged Misty. Stick to business. He went to the kitchen for the dessert and heard Raymond say, "Well, you know the saying–you scratch my back, I'll scratch yours."

Scratch her back, scum, and I'll break yours.

Misty shuddered. Raymond had never said anything suggestive to her before.

Gene emerged from the kitchen, removed the entree plates, and slipped a caramelized flan in front of each of them.

"Lovely," Misty exclaimed

"Yes, you are, dear," Raymond said. "I never realized quite how lovely."

Misty dropped her spoon, her eyes widening. Too late she realized her mistake. She should never have invited him to her apartment. Understandably, he had mistaken her motives and she was in a quandary as to how to right the wrong she had committed.

"We've known each other for many years, and now you've provided the perfect opportunity for us to get to know each other much better." He rose, stepped to Misty's side of the table, and grasped her wrist.

On his way back to the kitchen with a tray of dirty dishes, Gene halted. He didn't like the sound of what was happening. He made an about face.

"Oh, the dessert!" Misty said in a vain effort to distract Raymond.

"I have another dessert in mind." Raymond grasped her other wrist and drew her to a standing position.

Heart pounding, Misty said, "No, Raymond. This isn't what I had in mind."

"I'm sorry to hear that. But you have a loan in mind, and no collateral. Perhaps we could make some arrangements." He fastened his arms around her and pulled her close to him.

That crumb expected sex in exchange for a loan, Gene thought, enraged.

Feeling like a caged animal, Misty pressed her closed fists firmly against Raymond's chest. "No, Raymond!" She glanced at Gene who stood nearby, his face blazing.

"Don't pay any attention to him," Raymond ordered as he lowered his head to kiss her neck. "He's only a servant."

Gene released the tray. Dirty dishes clattered to the carpet. "That does it, creep. Let her go."

Raymond released Misty and whirled around to face his adversary. "Stay out of this."

"Maybe you didn't understand. The lady said 'No.'"

Raymond scowled. "I give you fair warning. I've got a black belt."

Gene glowered. "And I've got serrated teeth. Now do you want to leave under your own power or do you want me to be the machinery that makes it happen?"

Gasping, Misty entreated, "Oh, please gentlemen! We can settle this peaceably."

Ignoring her anguish, Raymond emitted a shrill, piercing sound.

Histrionics, Gene thought with disgust.

Eyes narrow, Raymond reared back into a ready stance, his right foot firmly planted, his left knee bent, toe on the ground. He held his left hand in a defensive position in front of his face and his right hand to the side of his head, prepared to strike.

Gene sighed, then shrugged. "Oh, hell." He forced a low guttural noise from his throat and feigned a forward movement. Immediately, Raymond thrust his rear leg forward to a front kick, aiming at Gene's solar plexus. Gene caught the foot in mid-kick. He twisted it to the left. Raymond fell to the right as Gene brought his foot to the groin of Raymond's splayed leg.

"No!" Misty shrieked, slapping her hands to her cheeks.

Crumpling, Raymond covered his crotch with his hands.

Seizing his advantage, Gene grasped the moaning

man by the seat of the pants and the scruff of the neck and hoisted him up.

"Open the door," he ordered. When Misty hesitated, he bellowed, "Now!" She complied.

"Don't hurt him!" she cried frantically.

"I'll have you for assault and battery," Raymond moaned, his toes skimming the floor.

Gene heaved him over the threshold.

Chapter 2

Gene slammed the door shut. Misty grasped the knob, struggling to reopen it. Gene leaned a flat palm against the door.

"He's hurt," Misty protested.

"Yeah, he hurts, but it won't last forever. He'll live."

When she persisted in her efforts to open the door, he said, "He's not worth it."

She stared defiantly into his eyes. "Don't be so pompous! He was my only hope for a loan."

"Nobody needs money that bad."

She pounded on the door with her fist. "How dare you! It wasn't just the money. He's an old friend."

Incredulous, he shook his head. "Friend? What kind of friend forces you into the bedroom?"

She faltered, taking a step back. "He wouldn't have...he couldn't have...." She squared her shoulders. "I could have handled him."

"Didn't look that way to me."

"You weren't saving me," she accused. "You detested Raymond from the moment you saw him."

27

Gene cringed at the element of truth in that statement. "Talk about pompous," he said dryly.

Misty turned toward the door and dropped her forehead against the cold wood. She sniffed loudly while reliving the traumatic experience of the past few moments. Her shoulders heaved and her body shuddered.

Fixing his gaze on the back of her lucent head of hair, Gene reached around her slight but curvaceous frame to hand her a linen napkin. "Here—use this."

Quivering, she accepted the cloth, dabbed at her eyes, then blew her nose. Gasping, she inhaled noisily, like a child with croup.

"Hey—you're better off without the creep."

"I...I know," she sobbed. "Sorry for yelling at you. I know you were just trying to help me."

He ran his hand across her back in a warm, comforting gesture. "You'll find another way to get your business going."

She shook her head, then pivoted, burying her forehead against Gene's massive chest. "I was wrong to have invited him here. But I've known him almost all my life and we've never been romantically involved. It never occurred to me I'd have to fight him off."

He wrapped his arms around her, massaging her neck with one hand. "*Hmmm, hmmm*," he hummed.

The warmth and strength of his hand eased the tension from her neck and torso. "If you hadn't been here..." Her voice trailed off as if the consequences of his absence were too ghastly to contemplate.

"But I was here." He felt her taut muscles soften.

"Surely he wouldn't have forced me. I just can't believe that. He must have been putting on a show." She turned her head to rest her cheek against Gene's chest and was further soothed by the feel and sound of the rhythmic beating of his heart. She felt sheltered in its strength.

He touched his lips to her gleaming hair and inhaled its fresh scent. He found himself humming the song *Unforgettable* that played on the CD, a perfect blend of Natalie and Nat King Cole's voices.

Misty's arms traveled to his back. She closed her eyes. His generous, well-muscled arms tightened around her. He started moving in rhythm to the music and she followed as if they were one being.

Mesmerized by the vibration of his humming, she snuggled closer, nesting in his bulk. The gentle strength of his arms rendered her secure from anxiety and harm. The moment was forever.

Holding her, Gene's emotions grazed from protector to lover. The two are not necessarily incompatible, he reasoned. If he pressed her closer, touching her curves and planes, he wondered if she would mold to him. He sensed she would. There's a fine line between comfort and passion. He felt he could easily erase it.

Yet, he hesitated. If he took advantage of her vulnerable state, there'd be little difference between him and that dirt bag Raymond. He resolved to remain in the role of comforter.

When the song ended, Misty lifted her head, an appealing weak smile curling her full lips. His resolve faltering, Gene dipped his head, brushing his lips across hers. Her lids languidly lowered. He placed his hands on either side of her head and gently pressed his lips against hers.

The door burst open. Gene and Misty started. With arms still about each other, they turned to face a wide-eyed, open-mouthed Lorna.

Her mind muddled as if she had been jolted awake from a drugged sleep, Misty swallowed then dropped her hands to her sides. "Uh, Lorna...this is Gene."

"So I see," her roommate replied icily.

Embarrassed by her situation, Misty felt foolish having gone from fighting off Raymond's unwelcome advances to melting into this man's arms, all within the period of less than an hour. She turned toward Gene. "And, *um*, this is my roommate Lorna."

Lorna stood motionless, as if transfixed by the scene before her.

With a casual wave of his hand, Gene muttered, "Hi, there." Reluctantly, he released Misty and headed toward the broken dishes on the carpet. "Better get this cleaned up," he mumbled.

"I'll help." On unsteady legs, Misty walked to the table in the living room and busied herself. "Would you like some flan, Lorna?"

In answer, her roommate fled to her bedroom and slammed the door.

Bewildered, Gene asked, "What's her problem?"

Misty's cheeks heated. "I don't know." But she had a good idea. Lorna had seen Gene first, had been immediately smitten by the hunk, and had overtly flirted with him. Now she walks into her apartment to find the object of her desire entwined in her roommate's arms. Lorna must feel betrayed, Misty thought dejectedly.

"Maybe an argument with her boyfriend," Gene offered. "So she was upset seeing us kiss." The kiss disturbed him, too. He wanted to continue from where they had left off, but the mood was broken. He was certain she'd resist. He smiled inwardly, thinking he'd create another mood at another time.

"Maybe," Misty responded. Cups rattled on saucers when she picked them up. She'd have to explain this situation to Lorna later. First, she'd have to explain her behavior to herself. Why would she react to this stranger so intimately? Was she forever destined to fall for self-centered, gorgeous men? No, she wouldn't allow it.

The two dishes of flan caught her eye. "How about eating this dessert? It looks scrumptious."

Gene gazed into her dark eyes, his arms still remembering the feel of her in them. "I'm surprised you want dessert. You didn't seem hungry this evening." He added with a wry grin, "It couldn't have been my cooking."

She shook her head. "Your cooking was superb. Raymond spoiled my appetite, but he's gone now." She didn't add that Gene aroused a different appetite. Instead, she took a mouthful of the cool, custard dessert and enjoyed the feel of it sliding down her throat. "It's wonderful," she murmured.

Watching her slip another spoonful of flan over her tongue, Gene felt his throat tighten. His own flan was difficult to swallow.

The dessert polished off, they finished cleaning and packing up his materials. Gene considered a friendly, good-bye kiss, but Lorna chose that moment to emerge from her bedroom, her eyes downcast. "Can I help you guys?"

"You're just in time," Misty responded in a sarcastic tone. "We're all finished." She located her checkbook. "I hope a check will do," she said to Gene. "I don't have cash."

"Hey–can't remember when I had such an exciting evening. It's on the house."

She stiffened. Was he exchanging his services for kissing her or because she had provided Raymond as a stuffed toy for him to kick around? His ego must have been well fed this evening, she surmised. "I prefer to pay for your services."

He shrugged, accepting the check. "Have it your way." He picked up his first load of equipment and started for the door.

"Let me help." Lorna quickly gathered his remaining foodstuffs and followed him out the door.

Misty heard the engine fire and the car drive off. Apprehensive about Lorna's potential reaction, she continued to work in the kitchen.

When Lorna returned, she stood watching Misty, then folded her arms on her chest. "Eventually you'll have to stop washing that stove."

Misty rinsed the sponge and squeezed it. "Well, what are you so upset about?"

"You were kissing him."

Misty was upset about that, too, but for a different reason. "So?" she responded defensively.

"So he's the divine creature *I* was flirting with. I saw him first."

"That doesn't mean he belongs to you. Besides, I didn't flirt with him. And I didn't mean to kiss him. It just sort of...well...happened."

Lorna puckered an eyebrow and unfolded her arms. "I guess my reaction was pretty immature."

Misty silently agreed.

With a grin, Lorna asked, "How about telling me just how the kiss did happen?" She glanced around the apartment. "And what happened to Raymond?"

Grateful to have the tension relieved, Misty mirrored her friend's smile. "All right. I'll make some tea and we'll talk."

The story told, Lorna pursed her lips indignantly. "I told you that Raymond has an evil gleam in his eye. You should report him to the police."

"For what? Being kicked below the belt and tossed out the door? I don't think so."

"I wish I could have seen that!" Lorna laughed, then with dancing eyes said, "Now tell me about Gene. Where do you see this romance leading?"

"There's no romance." Misty impatiently tapped her spoon against her cup. "I've told you I'm on my own for the first time in my life. I want it to stay that way, with no romantic entanglements." *Especially with yet another beautiful man,* she silently added.

"How can you say you haven't been on your own when you're a college graduate, taught school for a year, and spent two years in the Peace Corps?"

Thoughtful, Misty stirred her tea. "I lived at home when I was in college and teaching. My mother took care of my every need. She even ironed my clothes for heaven sakes." Misty shook her head, a rueful smile on her lips. "Sure I was away from home in the Peace Corps, but I had the very comforting assurance that whatever fate befell me, I'd be taken care of. The U.S. Government sort of replaced Mother."

Lorna's sparkling eyes widened. "So Gene's really fair game?"

"Absolutely," Misty said with assurance. With unease what she actually felt was a pair of sensual arms enveloping her and a muscular, masculine heart beating rhythmically next to her welcoming ear.

"Okay, Ms. Independence," Lorna continued, "in the absence of Raymond's loan, what's 'Plan B?'"

Misty's brows knitted. "The money from the model home job will carry me for a while."

Lorna set her mug on the table. "We need a receptionist-file clerk at my office."

"I appreciate the tip, Lorna, and I may have to resort to that, but for now I want to struggle along to see if I can support myself doing what I love to do."

"How about teaching more evening classes?"

Misty thought of her group of students–all adult women–who gathered at the local high school on Wednesday evenings to learn flower arranging. She considered teaching dried flower arranging, too. Decorative wreaths and mobiles might be of interest also, especially around holiday themes. She sighed. That wouldn't satisfy her urge to create unique arrangements for individual clients' homes, but it would keep beans on the table.

Gene regarded his buddy, Dave Arnel, who stared into the deli's glass case. He's about to complain again about my lack of junk food, Gene surmised.

"No doughnuts? What kind of a phony bakery is this?"

Dave, a well-muscled five feet nine inches, stood about three inches shorter than Gene. He had dark, wavy hair with a sharp widow's peak, and a constant five o'clock shadow.

"I do specialty cakes," Gene explained, as if speaking to an unreasonable child. "As you well know, I carry no other pastries."

"Never heard of a bakery without pastries."

"Just thinking of your cholesterol level, Dave. Some day you'll thank me for saving your life." Gene sliced through an apple and commenced chopping.

Dave emitted a disgusted sigh. "I wanted to take something to Julie. You know, sweets for the sweet."

Gene pictured Dave's girlfriend, Julie, a petite brunette, whose short locks curled unmanageably. *Not like Misty's sleek, smooth hair.*

"I have just the thing. A fresh fruit salad. Julie will love it–and you–for being so thoughtful. Trust me."

"Maybe you're right. She's always complaining about being too hippy." He paused, then grinned wickedly. "But I like her hips just the way they are."

"Then help her keep them that way," Gene said as he scooped mixed fruit salad into a container. "You don't want doughnuts on them."

"That's true. And how's your love life these days?"

Gene raised his knife and whacked into a banana. Dave was forever bugging him about his long workdays and lack of a social life. "Isn't it time for you to open your clip joint?" he responded.

"Sorry, but your tactics won't work. Insulting my tonsorial artistry won't stop me from asking the same question again."

Gene shrugged. "Don't have much time for that sort of thing. I need to get this business firmly established." He paused thoughtfully. "Although I did meet an interesting girl recently. She hired me to do a *Dinner For Two*."

"And?" Dave demanded. "Go on."

"And nothing. I haven't seen her since."

"Why not? Why don't you call her?"

"As a matter of fact, I'm going to call her today. The check she paid me with bounced. So much for a character reference."

"Those things happen," Dave said. "A check of mine bounced once. I had made a simple mathematical error in my checkbook." He picked up his carton of fruit salad. "Don't be too quick to judge her."

"Sure, Dave. Say 'Hi' to Julie."

Whistling *Unforgettable,* Dave sauntered out the door.

Now why did he pick that tune to whistle? Gene dropped his knife, rinsed off his hands, dried them, then picked up the telephone receiver. He punched in Misty's number. After her insistence on paying him, he wasn't going to let her get away with writing a phony check.

"Hello?" she answered.

That unforgettable voice again. "Your check bounced," he said without preliminaries.

Misty recognized his resonant voice. He sounded...what...irritated, agitated? She pictured his ruddy complexion deepening in color.

"I'm so sorry. I should have called you. I deposited a check in my account that bounced." *A large check I was counting on carrying me for a couple of months.* Quivering with anger, she recalled the man who had hired her to do the model home job.

He detected the quiver in her voice. He hoped she wasn't going to burst into tears. Suddenly, he was sorry he'd called. He should have just let it pass. "It's okay. Like I said before, it's on the house."

Between the *Dinner For Two* fiasco, the bounced check, and her lack of steady employment, Misty felt like she'd been on a financial and emotional roller coaster. She squared her shoulders. "No, I won't allow that. I insist on paying you. If I'm not paid again with a check that's good, I'm going to the police."

"Yeah, well, that'll take awhile, so don't worry about it."

"Believe me, Mr. Haynes, uh, Gene, I'm good for it."

"Sure. I've got to go now. The lunch crowd is showing up and unfortunately my help didn't." He hung up. Crowd wasn't a word he'd normally use to describe his lunch business. But a group of four and two groups of three just entered, looking the way harried people look on their lunch hour. He knew he'd have to serve them fast so they could get back to their jobs.

As usual, a few singles wandered in wanting take-out food. The grounds around the State Capitol were a favorite spot for picnicking and relaxing during lunch breaks.

Sam had been late before, but this was the first time he hadn't shown up at all. Ironic, Gene thought, on this my busiest day to date. Well, Sam was finished. Gene had the last he was going to take of that glib-tongued irresponsible excuse for help.

Momentarily, Gene considered putting an ad in the paper for part-time help, but dismissed the idea because he didn't have time to interview a bunch of people. Maybe a sign in the window would do it. He'd take the first person who walked through the door who appeared clean and ambitious.

Half an hour later, Gene felt schizophrenic as he took orders, prepared, and served lunches. He almost groaned when the door swung open. He couldn't believe he was in a situation where he actually didn't want any more customers. He glanced up and startled at the sight of Misty. Lovely as she is, I can't deal with her now, he thought. She appeared to be inspecting the place. He felt suddenly vulnerable having her see him out of control and with every surface piled with dirty dishes.

"...and iced tea," a customer was saying.

Gene's attention snapped back to his work. "Right away."

He turned to fill the order in time to see Misty pick a tray off the counter, then stack it with soiled dishes. She carried the load to the kitchen while his eyes followed the movements of her gently rounded hips. *I really don't have time for this.*

When Misty emerged from the kitchen, she halted in front of Gene, and with a dazzling smile, asked, "Do you have an apron?"

Wordlessly, he reached under the counter, picked up a starched white apron, and handed it to her.

"Thanks." She donned it.

For the next two hours, Gene stayed behind the counter preparing lunches and collecting tabs while Misty waited tables. Their only conversation was in regard to orders. But Gene watched her covertly. She was wearing blue slacks, or maybe they were purple–he couldn't tell the difference. Anyway, her blouse was about the same color–although he could have been wrong about that, too– but made of a silky, slinky material. Her gleaming black hair was pulled into a wide clip on the crown of her head and gentle waves cascaded in a fall, caressing her shoulders.

With an easy smile, she was friendly yet professional with the customers. Her skill and efficiency told him she'd waited tables before.

By two o'clock, the streaming customers had slowed to a trickle. Gene emerged from behind the counter to talk with Misty who was energetically wiping a table.

"I don't mean to look a gift horse in the mouth," he said, "but what's a nice girl like you doing in a place like this?"

Misty stopped wiping and frankly stared into his liquid green eyes as if she were genuinely astonished. "Horrors! You just managed two clichés in one sentence."

A grin took possession of his face. "Shall I try for three or will you talk?"

"No, please, no more!" She covered her heart with her hands as if in pain. "I'll talk, I'll talk!"

His stomach growled. "How about talking over lunch?"

"I accept. Pastrami on rye, please."

He regarded her with wrinkled brow. "You want to eat a cliché? No way. I'll fix us one of my specials."

Eyes alight, her taste buds came to attention in gastronomic anticipation. Gene served one more take-out customer, then prepared a lunch of Quiche Lorraine, a green salad, roll, and cheesecake for dessert. He whisked a cloth over a table for two, seated Misty, then served the meal. He sat next to her. As she started to take a bite of quiche, he gently grasped her wrist to halt the upward progression of her fork. "Talk first."

"Okay." She rested her wrist on the table, his hand still covering it. "You said on the telephone your help didn't show up. I owe you one. Actually, more than one, so I decided to drop over to see if I could be of some assistance."

He released her arm. "Your timing was perfect. This was the busiest lunch I've ever had."

"And the tastiest quiche I've ever had. *Hmm.* Seasoned to perfection."

"Thanks," he said, confused by his pleasure over her opinion of his cooking.

"What happened to your employee?"

Gene clenched his teeth. "Didn't show. He's through. I need reliable help. You've obviously done waitressing before."

"Serving," she corrected. "When I was in college."

He hesitated, contemplating her lack of employment. She wouldn't want to work here on a steady basis, he reasoned, but there's no harm in asking. "This isn't exactly the job of choice for a college graduate, but if you want a part-time job here, it's yours."

She swallowed another bite of quiche. "The hours?"

"I'm open from ten to five. I'd want you from eleven to three." *Maybe after hours, too.*

She glanced around the room, taking in the plainness of it, especially the stark white walls. Her mind raced ahead. The place definitely had possibilities. So did the owner, but she quelled that notion. "I'll take the job. But on one condition. I'll accept only half wages until my debt to you is paid off."

"That's not necessary."

"But that's my condition."

He shrugged in resignation. No sense in arguing with

41

her. "It's a deal."

She dug in her pocket, extracted bills and coins, and placed them on the table. "Here are today's tips. You had already waited on some of these customers before I arrived."

He raised his hand in protest. "Hey, no way. You earned that. More than that. I'll go for the half wages for now, but you keep the tips."

"Fair enough." She inhaled deeply, trying to draw in courage. "One other thing...um, what happened at my place." She stared at her cheesecake. "That wasn't exactly my typical behavior."

"Not mine, either. I mean, I don't throw bums out on a regular basis."

"That's not what I was referring to." She almost added, *And you know it*, but decided against it. "I meant I don't melt into a man's arms the first time I meet him."

He stifled a grin at her discomfort, glad she had melted into his arms, and looking forward to a repeat performance. "You had a bad night."

"Thanks for understanding. Of course, my point is, I think that since we'll be working together we should be sure there's no repeat of that kind of behavior."

He nodded as if in agreement, but his instincts told him otherwise.

"Have you heard from the bum?" he asked.

"Raymond? He's left messages on my recorder, but I haven't returned his calls." She took another bite of quiche. "If you want, you can feed me a lunch like this every day."

"Let's shake on the deal." He extended his hand. She slipped hers into it. He shook it, resisting the impulse to draw her fingers to his lips.

The next morning, Misty arrived at the deli at nine-thirty. The door was locked and the mini-blinds closed, so she rapped.

In the midst of food preparations, Gene was tempted to ignore whoever was at the front door. But it might be Dave with a bag of doughnuts wanting a cup of coffee to go with them. Gene started for the door when the knocking sounded again. Too delicate for Dave, he thought. He parted the blinds to peer out. Misty's sleek, gleaming hair tumbled uninhibited to her shoulder blades. Her cheeks were pinked with the cool morning air. She looked delicious. He opened the door. She carried a box that required both of her arms to manage and she wore an enigmatic smile that puzzled him and made him wary.

"I like employees who are early, but this is ridiculous."

She crossed the threshold. "I wanted to have time to place these before your customers started arriving."

Suspicious, he asked, "Place what?"

She set the box on a table. "Oh, just a few things to liven up the place. You know, to make it more aesthetically pleasing."

Her presence pleased him aesthetically, but he didn't want her disrupting his deli. "What's in the box?"

"A few things from home. You saw some of them on my walls. Your walls are so plain that I thought some decorating would help."

Gene shook his head. "No way. You're not messing up my freshly painted walls."

She raised an eyebrow. "But you admired my arrangements!"

His gaze grazed her from head to toe. Yes, he admired her arrangements. "Sure, in your place. But not here."

She tilted her head, her heart picking up speed from his frank appraisal of her form. "They'll make the food taste better."

He smiled at hearing her repeat the words he'd spoken at her apartment about a fire making the food taste better.

"I won't need your help," Misty added quickly. "Just go ahead and continue doing whatever it was you were doing."

He examined the contents of the box. The arrangements were attractive, he admitted. Maybe she was right. His walls were clean, but stark white. "Only a few," he said.

"Of course. Just a few."

With misgivings, he returned to the counter and resumed lunch preparations. But he found Misty distracting, and in spite of himself, glanced at her frequently. She surveyed the walls like an artist about to paint a mural. She laid the arrangements out on the tables, as if she were mentally fastening them to her palette. She disappeared into the restroom and returned with her hair twisted into a knot and pinned to the back of her head. Then she carried a chair and the first arrangement to the wall. Gene forced his attention back to the saffron rice salad he was preparing.

At quarter past eleven, Sam entered through the back door. He glanced at the dried arrangements and the girl tacking one to the wall. "Hey, what's up? You hired a decorator?"

Gene didn't answer immediately; instead, he savored the pleasurable anticipation of firing the over-fed weasel. "You sick yesterday?" he asked.

"Nah. A few of us went out for a beer after truck driving school and, well, we just sorta' lost track of time. You know how it goes."

"Sure, I know. Sam, I'd like you to meet Misty."

Standing on a chair tapping a fastener into the wall, she turned, and with a smile acknowledged the newcomer.

Nodding, Sam returned the smile. "You're makin' the place look pretty special."

"Thank you."

Bursting with his announcement, Gene finally blurted out, "Misty's not only my decorator, she's my new waitress."

"Server," she corrected, stepping off the chair.

"You think you got so much business now you need extra help?"

Gene smiled wickedly. "No, I need only one reliable server."

Eyes narrowed to slits, Sam nodded. "Oh, I get it."

"I was confident it wouldn't take you long."

Sam's face turned a blotchy red. "Well, you can take

this crummy job and shove it." He strode toward the door.

Inwardly grinning, Gene called out, "How about a pastrami on rye before you leave?"

Sam halted in mid-stride.

"On the house," he added.

Gene visualized the war going on within his former employee. Sam was torn between the desire to derive satisfaction from a theatrical exit or the pleasure of filling his belly. He hesitated indecisively.

"Consider it severance pay," Gene added.

The belly won. "Yeah. You owe me that."

Gene winked at Misty.

Misty gazed in wonder and longing at Gene's powerful forearm as he served them each *cordon blu*, his lunch special on this, her third day of employment at the deli. She wanted to reach out and stroke the curly russet down on his arm. Instead she slid her gaze to the plate in front of her from which enticing aromas arose.

With the delicacy befitting the finest French chef, Gene gently spooned a white sauce flecked with green herbs over the chicken. Rice with bits of mushroom nestled next to the main dish while elegant asparagus tips with a hollandaise sauce and colorful bits of pimento lounged nearby.

"Your meals are a work of art," she commented enthusiastically. "The colors are subtle, complimented by sparks of brightness. How do you decide what colors to use?"

Gene cleared his throat. "Um, just what I think will go well together." He took the seat next to her, his knee brushing against hers. She twitched.

"Every dish is seasoned to perfection," she murmured.

He nodded, accepting the compliment. "It's the fresh herbs. They make a big difference. I used to grow my own, but now I buy them from a woman who has a backyard herb farm."

"Tell me about when you grew your own herbs."

He took a bite of chicken and chewed thoughtfully. "I was a forest ranger in Yosemite's high country. A pretty isolated spot. For entertainment I collected books on growing and cooking with herbs."

"And you practiced," she added.

"And I practiced." He didn't add that not only did he enjoy the products of his avocation, but he found that inviting female backpackers to his cabin resulted in their great admiration of his culinary expertise, thereby enhancing after-dinner romancing. He wondered how greatly Misty admired his culinary expertise. Not greatly enough, he feared.

"How did you get from Yosemite to Sacramento?"

"Got tired of my isolated existence. Decided to see if I could turn my hobby into a livelihood, so I bought this place. I camp out in the back room."

She had wandered into his bedroom by mistake the day before. Neat and orderly, it was decorated in black and white. Stark, yet inviting. She had lingered only a moment before abruptly turning to leave. It was too intimate a place.

"Is twelve your usual number of lunch patrons?"

"That's up from six."

"That won't do at all. Of course two women came in today just because they saw my arrangements on the wall." She cut into her chicken.

"Yes, I know. Your were quick to point that out." He buttered a roll. "But I don't think this is going to work. They bought one of the arrangements and now the money in the till is mixed up."

"No problem. Just write my sales on a separate sheet and we'll settle later."

He frowned. "This is a deli, not a craft shop."

"Uh huh," she answered, savoring the asparagus. "You will recall that the ladies also bought your special for their dinners." She wanted to tell him about the mobiles she was fashioning to hang from the ceiling, but decided the time wasn't quite right.

"So you think you're going to increase my business." He resented her intrusion, but admitted to himself the place did look better. Plus, the decorations gave the patrons something to admire and talk about while they were waiting to be served.

"Yes, that's possible. My arrangements might bring them in, but of course when they sample your cuisine, they'll be back for more."

His skin crawled. Now she was attempting to worm her way into his business by flattering him. In spite of her sultry voice, he wouldn't fall for a line like that.

The front door opened with a "whoosh" and Lorna exploded through. "Raymond's on the warpath," she exclaimed.

Chapter 3

"Can't she open a door and walk through it like a normal person?" Gene grumbled.

Ignoring him, Misty turned to her roommate. "What's Raymond up to?"

Breathless, Lorna pulled a chair up to their table and flopped down. "Whew!" She gazed wistfully at their food.

Gene cleared his throat. "You wouldn't want some lunch, would you?"

"If it's not too much trouble. You see, I had two hours off between demonstrations–" She looked at Gene with doe eyes. "I demonstrate vacuum cleaners at department stores. Anyway, I went home for lunch and the phone rang."

Gene rose to prepare her lunch. "I'll bet it was Raymond."

"How did you know?" Not waiting for an answer, she continued: "He asked for you, Misty. He almost demanded to know where you were!" She paused for a breath. "So of course I didn't bother to eat lunch. I just

49

came straight over here."

Misty's eyes widened with alarm. "You didn't tell him."

"I told him off is what I told him. I said he had no business knowing where you were." She folded her arms across her chest. "Then he said he filed a complaint with the police. I told him to just try it." She gave her head a satisfied nod.

Bewildered by Lorna's last utterance, Gene slowly turned his head, hoping her statement would fall into place, like a billiard ball into a pocket.

"He's bluffing," Misty said. "Raymond knows I'd tell the police Gene was protecting me. He doesn't stand a chance of having any charges stick, even with a pricey lawyer."

"Right," Gene agreed. "Besides, if he'd contacted the police, they have been here by now."

Smiling and sniffing, Lorna was distracted by the lunch Gene placed before her.

Misty frowned. "But why would Raymond even threaten to go to the police?"

"Simple. He wants your attention." Gene realized he didn't want Misty to give any of her attention to Raymond. "Don't give it to him," he added.

"This is wonderful," Lorna exclaimed, while looking at Gene and fluttering her eyelashes. "I'll tell all my friends and co-workers about your food."

"Do that."

"I won't give Raymond the time of day," Misty said, rising. "Now if you'll excuse me, I need to go home to prepare for my class this evening."

"What's your subject tonight?" Lorna queried.

"Japanese flower arranging." Misty picked up her purse, slung the strap over her shoulder, and was gone.

She doesn't even care about leaving me alone with her flirting roommate, Gene mused. Irked, he wondered why that should bother him.

Misty surveyed the ten eager faces, the twenty bright eyes expectantly awaiting the evening's entertainment. She wondered if her lesson plan was interesting enough to hold their attention. Familiar stage fright inexorably seeped through her extra-strength antiperspirant.

Intellectually, she realized she had nothing to be anxious about. She knew her subject well. Yet, until she plunged in and got actively involved in the teaching-learning process, she felt like a poorly rehearsed understudy. If Gene were lecturing on French cuisine, she knew he wouldn't be a pinch anxious–rather, he would exude self-assurance. Of course, his magnificent body alone would command attention and respect. On the other hand, she reasoned, her appearance was feminine and complimentary to her subject of flower arranging. Yet, in spite of all her teaching experience both in and out of the Peace Corp, when she first stood before a class of adults she couldn't shake the ridiculous notion of breaking into a song and dance routine.

"Ikebana is the Japanese art of flower arrangement," Misty began. "More precisely, the word Ikebana means the arrangement of living plant material. Japanese arrangements often have a paucity of flowers."

"Excuse me!" Mrs. Anderson waved a plump hand.

This wasn't the first time the talkative woman had interrupted. She never seemed satisfied unless she was the center of attention. "Yes?"

"Is it proper for a lady to give flowers to a gentleman?"

"Why, yes, of course."

This brought murmurs of agreement from the group.

One woman said, "I send a rose to my husband on every anniversary."

"The last time we had an argument," offered another, "I sent flowers to my husband at work." The other women laughed.

"Since my name's Tulip," giggled the youngest in the group, "I sent a tulip to a guy I like. No note." She blushed and regarded the floor. "But he guessed and we're going out Saturday night."

"So there you have it," Misty said, hoping to finalize the discussion. Alas, Mrs. Anderson had only just begun.

"What kind of flowers do you think would be suitable for saying 'thank you' to a gentleman whose creativity simply made your party?" She hesitated, then with downcast eyes, quickly added, "There's no romantic attachment, of course."

Who's she trying to fool? Mrs. Anderson obviously had a crush on someone. And it wasn't her husband.

"How about using your own creativity?" Misty suggested. "Instead of purchasing a flower arrangement, do your own."

"Oh, do you really think I could carry it off?"

"Of course. You've learned skills in this class–"

"What a perfectly lovely idea! I'll do it."

"Good. That's settled then," she said, hoping to finalize the discussion.

Misty placed a low ceramic vase on the demonstration table. "The container you choose for Japanese arrangements must always be in harmony with the total composition. An ideal Japanese arrangement might employ a bud, a half-opened bud, and one flower in bloom." She placed daffodils, off center, as she spoke. "This represents the past, the present, and the future."

After demonstrating the art of bending branches, she announced, "Now it's your turn." The students assembled their materials. The rest of the evening Misty circulated among the women, offering individual assistance and instruction as they completed their individual projects.

With closure, she gathered her materials together and Tulip helped her carry them to her car. Half an hour later, she eased into her parking slot at the apartment complex. Raymond emerged from the shadows. Misty gasped and checked to be sure her doors were locked.

He approached her and spoke through the closed window. "For heaven sakes, Misty, I'm not going to attack you!"

She cracked the window. "Then what are you doing skulking around in the shadows?"

"I'm not skulking. But you wouldn't answer my calls, so what choice did I have?"

"After your behavior at my apartment, can you blame

me?"

He placed his fists on his hips. "How about *your* behavior? I expected something else from you, too. And I don't mean sex. We've always been friends, and I thought that was what the evening was about. I mean, you're not exactly my type–er, that is, as I said, we've always been friends."

Misty felt a momentary twinge of guilt. Still, his behavior had been abominable.

"But when I saw that fancy–and for you–expensive set up," he added. "I thought you were coming on to me."

Misty quickly expelled the air from her lungs. She had to make peace with Raymond. Their families were old friends, after all. There was no way she could totally avoid the man. "I regret giving you the wrong impression, Raymond, but that didn't give you the right to force yourself on me. When a woman says 'No,' she means 'No!'"

"Okay. I apologize. Nevertheless, to find out that all you wanted from me was a loan wasn't exactly flattering. I admit I was a bit overbearing on purpose."

"Apology accepted," Misty said. She had difficulty meeting his eyes. After all, her motives had not been at all altruistic either. "I apologize, too."

Raymond relaxed his fists and let his arms fall to his sides. "Now why don't you get out of the car so we can talk?"

Misty glanced up to her apartment windows to see the lights on. Lorna was home. "Did you really make a report to the police?"

"No. I was just mad as hell."

She unlocked the car door and Raymond opened it.
"In that case, let's pretend the whole disastrous evening
never happened. Would you like a cup of coffee?"

Raymond hesitated. "You're not harboring that raw
side of beef in your apartment, are you?"

"You mean Gene? Of course not." *An interesting
idea, however.* She loaded Raymond's arms with her
teaching materials and he trailed her up the stairs, into the
apartment, and took a seat at the kitchen table.

"You home, Misty?" Lorna called. She emerged
from her bedroom wearing a mint green silky robe that
both contrasted with and complimented her blonde hair,
blue eyes, and light coloring. She halted abruptly at the
sight of Raymond. "Rapist! You invite rapists into our
home?"

Raymond rolled his eyes and gave a disgusted twist
to his lips.

"We've made our peace," Misty explained. "Mutual
excuses. Mutual apologies. The evening never happened.
Coffee will be ready in a minute. Please join us."

"Well, just so the telephone is near. In case I need to
call 9-1-1."

Raymond threw up his hands. "If you're wearing
your chastity belt, you're safe."

"Okay you two," Misty said. "We've negotiated one
peace this evening. We don't need another war."

With a wary eye on Raymond, Lorna cautiously
lowered herself into a chair. "But he hasn't explained his
behavior to me. After all, it was my roommate he was so

rude to."

"I notice you're not tainting yourself by speaking directly to me," Raymond groused. "Not that I owe you any explanations, but I will tell you how I felt about the situation. I thought I was being invited over for a friendly evening. When I discovered the real purpose for my presence, I admit I reacted by being a boor."

"You mean you were punishing Misty by forcing yourself on her?"

Raymond sighed. "Something like that. Pretending at least."

Lorna's disapproving features relaxed, her voice softening. "You wanted her to be as uncomfortable as you felt."

Raymond looked at Lorna as if seeing her for the first time. In a softer tone, he said, "You've stated my feeling exactly. I was a bit childish, I admit." He turned to Misty. "But surely you realize I wouldn't have played the Neanderthal and hauled you off to the bedroom."

Misty poured the coffee. "I was too upset and confused to think rationally."

Raymond balled his fists. "And then to have that untrained bear get the better of me…. Well, it was just too much."

Bear, Misty thought. Yes, snuggling against Gene was as warm and as comforting as a bear rug. Just thinking about him stirred emotions within her that were as frightening as if she had encountered a grizzly.

Raymond glanced at the sugar bowl. "Have any sugar substitute? My weight was up a pound today.

Played an extra game of tennis."

"Sorry, no," Misty responded.

"Well, I'll just use skim milk. You do have that, don't you?"

"It's all we use," Lorna offered. "We're careful about our bodies, too, even if we do have to work for a living and can't manage to play tennis every day."

"If you expect an apology because I'm wealthy, you'll be disappointed. I know what it's like not to have money, and believe me, having it is better." He stirred his coffee. Lorna stirred hers. "I've been thinking about that Victorian house, Misty–"

Misty raised her hands, palms up. "Please don't mention it, Raymond. I'm embarrassed I ever thought of asking you for a loan. It was a terrible blunder on my part. Remember, we agreed that the evening never happened." She dipped an Oreo into her coffee then took a bite.

"But it won't hurt if I look at it," he persisted. He sipped his coffee. Lorna sipped hers.

Misty thought wistfully of her shattered dream of operating her own business, and along with it her longing for true independence and self-reliance. But shattered or not, she'd pick up the pieces. She wouldn't lose sight of her goal. She'd work hard, save her money and eventually qualify for a business loan. "Please don't bother looking at the house, Raymond." She added a fib, "I'm not interested in it any longer."

"Then how will you support yourself?" He rested his right elbow on the table. Lorna set her left elbow on the table.

His question irritated Misty. It was really none of his business. "I'm working part-time for Gene and selling my arrangements in his deli."

"You're working for that–that thing?"

Ignoring his shock, she added milk to her coffee. "And of course I teach."

"And that's it?" He stared at Misty. Lorna stared at him.

"I'm doing wonderfully, Raymond. I appreciate your concern, but I don't need your help."

He shrugged. Lorna shrugged.

Misty's jaw slackened. Why, Lorna was mirroring Raymond's movements!

Dave dunked a glazed donut into his coffee. "So this girl's a terrific waitress, huh?"

"The correct term seems to be *server*," Gene responded as he snipped fresh dill into potato salad.

"Right. And I suppose she'd resent being called a *girl*." He polished off the glazed donut and selected a jelly-filled one.

"I suppose so."

"Is she a babe?"

"If by that you mean is she good looking? I'd say yes, she is attractive." *The understatement of the century.* Spending so much time with Misty without ever touching her kept him simmering like a stew. He wondered when he'd boil over.

"So tell me how things are going–has she succumbed

to your rugged charms?"

Gene shook his head. "Is that all you think about?"

"Of course not," Dave protested. "I think about fishing and backpacking, but my best buddy is too busy for those things these days." He bit into the doughnut, then peered reproachfully at the hole he'd just made. "What a gyp. There isn't a teaspoon of jelly in this one."

"Your dentist will be glad to hear that." Gene placed the salad in the refrigerator display case, then picked up a turkey breast and commenced slicing. "I'll make time for backpacking soon," he promised, and he meant it. He needed to take some time for himself. To be away from the deli. To be away from Misty. On the other hand, he wondered if she liked to backpack. He fantasized about making love to her under a blanket of stars. He'd been fantasizing about her a great deal of late.

"I'll hold you to that. Gotta get to work. Shaggy-headed customers will soon be beating a path to my door." He rose as the door opened and Misty entered. Gene introduced them. Dave gave her hand a hearty shake, then excused himself. He turned just before exiting, caught Gene's attention, and raised and lowered his eyebrows several times in quick succession.

Gene shook his head as if his friend were hopeless. But he stopped slicing in order to take in Misty's presence. Refreshing as lemon, she looked better to him than fresh basil tasted. She was staring at the Japanese flower arrangement perched atop the deli counter that Mrs. Anderson had brought in that morning.

"What creative thing did you do that 'simply made'

Mrs. Anderson's party?" she asked.

"You know Mrs. Anderson?"

"She's in my flower arranging class. She composed this Ikebana last night."

"Ah, she has a creative teacher. I like it. It inspired me to contemplate Asian. Next week we'll have a Japanese main dish."

Misty conjured up an image of the elderly, married Mrs. Anderson gushing over Gene. Revolting! It was also disgusting the way so many of the younger women who patronized the deli flirted openly with him. Some people have no pride, she decided. "You haven't answered my question. What inspired her to give it to you?"

"I decorated a cake with a murder scene for her murder-mystery party."

Misty donned an apron. "She has a wild crush on you, you know."

"Yes, I know," he said matter-of-factly, a sly grin on his face.

"And I suppose you encourage her attention to increase her patronage."

His response was drowned by the arrival of the first two customers. The arrival of three more patrons changed the focus of Misty's attention, and a slow but steady stream of customers kept her busy the next few hours.

Later, over a lunch of vegetable soufflé, Misty said, "Mrs. Anderson's composition inspired an idea in me."

Suspicious, Gene responded, "What's that?"

"Fresh flowers."

"Oh, no–not in my deli."

"But people might very well buy a rose to go with a take-out deli dinner."

Gene shook his head emphatically. "Not here they won't."

"You're not thinking creatively," she persisted. "You need to devise ways to increase business."

"I don't want the fragrance of fresh flowers warring with the aromas of my food."

"Oh…I hadn't thought of that. Perhaps you're right."

His face softened. Well, she can be reasonable, he thought. Beauty and reason. Good combination. Plus, he liked the way she relished his food. She didn't just move it around her plate and then leave half of it like her roommate. "How did you get into the flower business?" he asked.

"I grew up with flowers. My mother loved them–she still has a large flower garden. I majored in art in college with a minor in education." She hesitated.

"Yes?" he encouraged.

"I taught school for a year then did a two year stint in the Peace Corps. In South America. Now I want to have my own business. To be my own boss."

"Commendable." He paused. "What are you doing Sunday night?"

She looked at him sharply. "I thought I made it clear that our relationship was to remain strictly business." Yet her heart skipped at the thought that he would actually ask her for a date.

"You misunderstand." *Actually, she hadn't*

misunderstood. He'd like nothing better than to date her. Nothing, perhaps, except at this very moment kissing that smooth, soft spot below her left ear. "Mrs. Anderson has commissioned a *Dinner for Two* Sunday night for her husband's birthday."

She nodded, ignoring her twinge of disappointment. "Go on."

"Well…like you said, she's crazy about me." He ran his finger around the inside of his collar.

Why, he doesn't want to chance being alone with Mrs. Anderson! The thought that an elderly, plump, woman like Mrs. Anderson could cause anxiety for a man like Gene was a revelation to her. "Are you concerned her husband might not be there?"

"That would be the worst-case scenario. And it's happened."

Misty wanted to know what the rest of the evening was like when no man showed up.

"But barring her husband's absence," Gene continued, "she might make such a fuss over me that the unfortunate Mr. Anderson would be left out in the cold."

"I see." And for the first time, she did see that unwanted female attention could pose problems for the most virile of men. "You want me to chaperone," she quipped.

"You could call it that."

"But how would I fit into the evening's festivities?"

"Be my helper, my *sous chef,* if you please. It'll wipe out the rest of your debt."

That sounded good to Misty. She could use the

money.

"Actually," Gene continued, "I could use help at other times, too. Several times I've gotten calls for two dinners on the same evening, and I had to turn one down. If I could get one all set for you to serve, I could go do the other. Dinner at the Andersons could be your training ground."

Misty nodded in assent. Her mind raced ahead to the doors this new role could open. She would do arrangements for the dinners; perhaps news of her talent and availability would spread by word of mouth. She'd make extra money working evenings, also, and edge that much closer to her goal.

"Does that nod mean yes?" He hoped so. Then he'd know what she was doing weekend evenings instead of just wondering where she might be, what boyfriends she might have. Plus, he'd see more of her if she accepted his proposal. They'd be working closely together after dark…who knows what might develop?

"Yes, I'd like to try it."

"Good. Do you have black trousers or skirt and a white blouse you could wear?"

"You mean like a uniform?"

"That's the idea."

"Yes, I'm sure I do."

"You don't want to be dressed fancier than the woman you're serving," he explained. "And pull your hair into a bun." His gaze caressed her face. "Don't use makeup," he added.

"I'll be a real Plain Jane."

You'd need a bag over your head for that.

"Another perfect cake!" Mrs. Anderson clapped her hands together and brought them to her full cheeks in sheer ecstasy as she gazed at the scene Gene had created. Titled "The Nineteenth Hole," it depicted a man and woman seated on a couch holding hands before a roaring fire

"I enjoyed doing it. And it's filled with lemon custard, just as you requested."

"That's Jason's favorite."

Mrs. Anderson was gowned in a black sequined evening dress that hung in loose pleats from her shoulders to her knees, yet failed to conceal her many generous rolls of adipose tissue. She placed a soft, puffy hand on Gene's forearm.

"It's lovely having you in my home…so…so intimate."

He freed his arm by lifting his small round table, unfolding it, and setting it up, off-center, in the living room. "Yes, it is intimate for a couple to be served an elegant dinner in their own home."

She fastened him with a dreamy smile and lidded eyes. "And to be served by such an elegant gentleman."

He groaned inwardly, chastising himself. I should have insisted on picking up Misty instead of agreeing to meet her here, he thought. "You'll be served by an elegant lady, also. I have a helper coming."

She gasped, her jaw dropping. "A woman is coming here?"

"Yes. It's going to be a really special evening."

"But–" she sputtered, "but you didn't say anything about a helper. You don't need a helper! I can assist you." She pushed her lower lip up and out in a pouty gesture and again rested a hand on Gene's forearm.

He waved his arm, ridding himself of her hand. "Absolutely not. I wouldn't dream of having you work tonight, Mrs. Anderson. This evening is for you and Mr. Anderson to relax and to concentrate on each other."

The doorbell rang.

"I'll get it," Gene said, hastening to the door and eagerly opening it. "Welcome!" He smiled at Misty's attempt to look "plain." She wore black slacks and a white high-necked, long-sleeved cotton overblouse. Her raven's wing hair was bunned at the nape of her neck. With no discernible makeup, her fresh youthful complexion glowed invitingly. Her full lips shone and looked eminently kissable.

Startled by his hearty welcome, Misty whispered, "Is your virtue still intact, or am I too late?"

He frowned.

"Want me to give her a karate chop?"

Disturbed by her attempt to trivialize his predicament, he widened the door for her to enter. The women stood facing each other at opposite ends of the hallway. "I believe you two know each other."

Mrs. Anderson's face sagged. "Why, Ms. Jones!"

Attempting to ignore the shock and disappointment registered on Mrs. Anderson's face, Misty replied, "Good evening. I'm thrilled about helping you and your husband have a lovely birthday celebration."

"Well...my goodness, this is a...surprise." Mrs. Anderson extracted a lace handkerchief from her dress and fanned her forehead. "I do believe I'll rest until my husband comes home from golfing."

"You do that, Mrs. Anderson," Gene responded. "We can take care of everything here."

Mrs. Anderson shuffled to her bedroom.

"She wasn't exactly delighted to see me," Misty said.

"I didn't expect her to be."

"What can I do to help?"

"You can set the table. Everything you'll need is in the box on the couch."

Misty hastened to the box, selected an off-white round cloth, and covered the small table. She set out two placemats noticing a tag on each mat labeled "green." As she removed the tags, she thought of the signs Gene had around the deli lettered with color names. They struck her as peculiar, but she hadn't questioned him about them. Next, she placed the same China Gene had used for her disastrous *Dinner for Two*. She shuddered, recalling that two dinner plates from the set were broken when Gene came to her aid. Then she located the napkins. One was green, one was brown. The labeling tags on both read "green."

She returned to the kitchen. "There's one green and one brown napkin."

Gene glanced up from his dinner preparations. "What?" A familiar knot suddenly girded his stomach. He was in kindergarten. He drew a picture of a cow and colored it green. He thought it was brown. The other kids laughed.

Concerned, Misty couldn't read the expression on Gene's splendid face. Pain? Fear? But why, she puzzled. She repeated, "Both tags say green, but one napkin is brown."

He shook his head as if to dismiss the problem. "It'll just have to do. Dim the lights. Maybe they won't notice."

"All right." Still in a quandary, she returned her attention to setting the table. After placing the silverware and wine glasses, she set a small dried flower arrangement in the center and a candle on either side. She lit the candles, dimmed the lights, and went back to Gene. She watched him for a moment before speaking. The art of preparing food had never looked so masculine. "So what's on this evening's menu?"

"We'll start with fresh oyster mushrooms in a sherry cream sauce with French garlic toast. Chunks of melon on the side."

"*Mmm.*" She watched and learned as he gently stirred the contents of a saucepan. "Then what?"

"Medallions of beef over wild rice and a mosaic of sautéed vegetables in a wine sauce."

"Sounds heavenly." She had eaten before leaving the apartment, nevertheless, hunger pangs assaulted her.

Mrs. Anderson bustled in, appearing somewhat revitalized.

"I heard my husband driving into the garage. I want to answer the door myself." She waited a few moments then threw the door open as her husband reached the top step. "Surprise! Happy birthday, darling."

Slim as the golf bag slung over his shoulder, Mr. Anderson's flesh was stretched taut over his facial bones, his head covered by wisps of hair he had grown long on one side and flipped over his bald pate. His crown shown through like a freshly scrubbed golf ball. "What is this, Mabel?"

She threw her arms around his neck and stood on tiptoe to peck him on the lips. "We're going to have a lovely birthday celebration right here in our own home."

"This way, sir." Gene stepped forward, escorted Mr. Anderson to the couch, then uncorked and served champagne. He returned to the kitchen. "Serve the appetizers–" He stopped short when he saw that Misty had shrunk to the farthest corner of the kitchen, a panicked look on her face. "What the hell–"

She gestured wildly toward the living room. "That's Jason Anderson," she whispered hoarsely.

"Yes. He lives here."

"It never occurred to me he could be the same Anderson."

"Same as what?" Gene demanded.

"*Shh*! "He's the one who hired me for the model home job."

"You mean the rubber check writer?"

She nodded her head vigorously. "The same. If he recognizes me the evening will be ruined."

"You'd better get out of here. Fast. I'll serve the appetizers. You beat it."

Misty snatched her purse and headed for the front door, Gene following.

Jason Anderson chose this moment to glance toward the door. "Young woman," he bellowed.

Facing the door, Misty hesitated.

"Sorry, she has to go." Gene stepped in front of Misty, opened the door, and put his hand on the small of her back to hasten her departure.

Nostrils flaring, Mr. Anderson scurried out of the living room into the hall. "Just one minute! I recognize that woman."

Misty whirled around to face him. "How dare you–"

"How dare me? How dare you! How dare you enter my home after harassing my employees with your phone calls."

With every muscle taut, Misty's voice deepened and slowed. "Legitimate calls, Mr. Anderson. All I want is the money you owe me."

In the background, Mrs. Anderson clucked, "Oh, dear, oh, dear."

"I told you you'll get your check. You must be patient a bit longer."

Gene closed the door.

"Then you'll have to be patient with my calls," she challenged. "Why, you haven't even offered partial payment!"

He waggled his index finger at her. "That's no reason for you to call the Better Business Bureau. Now some of my employees fear our business is about to collapse. You're undermining my credibility."

"I'll undermine more than your credibility when I go to the police, which is exactly what I'll do if I don't receive payment in full."

His lips thinning to slivers of ice, Mr. Anderson took one step forward. "I'm warning you...."

Gene placed himself squarely between the two antagonists. "Watch your tongue, Mr. Anderson. There'll be no warnings and no threats to my *sous chef.*"

The slight man drew back at the sight of Gene's bulk and ruddy complexion, which was rapidly heating to a furious red.

Mr. Anderson waved both of his arms in the air. "This is my home, and I want the both of you out of here. Immediately!"

"Oh, dear," Mrs. Anderson moaned, "I just knew something dreadful would happen when I saw Ms. Jones arrive."

Gene nodded to Misty. "Pack the things in the kitchen." He strode to the living room, Mr. Anderson hot on his heels.

"I want you out NOW!"

Spinning around, Gene grabbed a generous amount of the man's Polo shirt and said, "I'm not leaving without my belongings." He backed the man toward the couch. "Now sit down and shut up before I lose my temper."

Mr. Anderson sat. Gene handed him a glass of champagne. Mrs. Anderson plopped down next to her husband and patted his knee.

Gene whisked the setting off the table, stacked the dishes in the box, then folded the table and shoved it under his arm. He walked to the kitchen. "You ready?" he asked Misty.

"Yes, I think so." Her voice quivered like a feather in a breeze.

He opened the door for her. "Meet me at the deli."

Chapter 4

"Dinner is served, Madam." Gene bowed at the waist, then rose and looked directly into Misty' dark, vacant eyes. He had been so busy salvaging the Andersons' dinner for the two of them to enjoy that he hadn't noticed how Misty stood, passively watching him while quivering like a rabbit. She's tough as round steak, he thought, yet delicate as a soufflé. He set down his spatula and went to her, circling her with both his arms. He resisted the urge–the need–to tighten the circle, to draw her closer.

"Talk to me." His voice sounded husky, as if it had battled to creep over his Adam's apple.

She sniffed. "I've ruined two of your dinners."

"It isn't ruined. We can eat it." He put gentle pressure on her head until her cheek rested against his chest.

"You know what I mean. You won't be paid for tonight. And think of the terrible PR I've generated for you."

"I don't mind." He brushed his lips against her

73

lemon-scented hair. "You know, you were really great tonight. You chomped that crumb off and chewed him up."

In spite of herself, a wry smile skewed her lips. Misty tilted her head to look up at Gene. "He all but foamed at the mouth," she said.

They both laughed, then suddenly quieted, their gazes searching for meaning in each other's eyes.

Gene dipped his head and brushed a gentle kiss across her lips. Like fresh, ripe berries. An appetizer. He hungered for more.

To Misty, Gene's lips felt full and gently, sweetly, abrasive. The delicate warmth of his kiss spread deliciously throughout her body.

Supposedly, she was striving to stand on her own two feet, yet once again she found herself enveloped and protected by him. He's being kind and considerate, she reasoned. He's trying to cheer me up.

With both hands against his broad chest, she pushed hard, freeing herself. "I've got to go," she said. She grabbed her purse and dashed out.

Gene watched her race out as if a predator were close on her heels. He walked to the window and peered through the blinds to be sure she made it safely to her car. The engine fired and she was off. "Why did she run?" he wondered. He could tell she enjoyed their physical contact. Maybe even as much as he did. His chest still felt the impression of her cuddled against him. Was she so adamant that their relationship remain strictly professional, or did something else bother her? He shrugged. It's just as well, he decided. They could easily grow too fond of each other and he couldn't off her what she deserved–a lasting relationship.

The enraged black stallion stretched vertically on its hind legs, its forelegs boxing the air. Humid, steaming wind belched from the bellows of its distended nostrils; coal button eyes skittered sideways to catch a glimpse of the feared, foreign burden on its back.

The boy held fast to the saddle, his left hand making a wild circle in the air. "Yahoo!" he whooped.

As a final touch, Gene placed a golden pole through the center of the carousel cake he had just fashioned for a boy's eighth birthday. The boy's mother had indicated that her son's favorite activities were rodeos and carnivals. Gene was satisfied that he had depicted both interests on the cake. He boxed and labeled it.

He burped. Having consumed both of the Anderson dinners the night before, he was still full. His morning jog had at least redistributed the meals.

He had found, however, that overstuffing his belly hadn't decreased his more primal urges. He'd also discovered that cold showers were overrated.

Misty breezed into the deli as if the night before had never happened. Gene smiled at the lovely picture she made. Her shimmering hair, coiled into a knot, perched high atop her head like a crown. Her dark slacks and light blouse skimmed her appealing curves like a delicate glaze on a Bavarian cream.

His attention was drawn away from her face and form

to the large cardboard box she carried. He frowned and, with a jaundiced eye, observed her and the box more closely.

"You're early again," he said suspiciously. "What do you have in the box?"

"Mobiles. You'll love them." She set the box on a table and unpacked her wares.

Returning to his mincing, he responded, "I'm not so sure."

"Don't worry. There's no fresh flowers in here." She glanced around the room. "You have a folding ladder in the back. I'll get it." She bustled out, reappeared, set up the ladder, climbed it, and tacked a mobile to the ceiling.

She was relieved and grateful that Gene hadn't mentioned her sudden departure the previous evening. He was behaving as if nothing had happened. To him, their show of affection meant no more than a casual hug, she reasoned.

Covertly, Gene watched her work. Each time she tacked a mobile she enthusiastically tilted her head to and fro in order to examine the dangling pieces from all angles. She was obviously pleased with her work. Gene wondered if he could ever spark the same delight in her.

"Do I smell crab?" she called down from her perch on the ladder.

"Fresh crab salad. Sam's driving a refrigerator truck for the Arctic Ocean Seafood Suppliers from Seattle to Sacramento, so we might be having more fresh shellfish in the future."

"Yummy." She descended and readjusted the ladder.

"Do you figure on dragging out that ladder every time someone wants to buy one of those things?"

"Things, you say? Things? Don't be gauche. They're works of art. Specifically, mobiles. All made from Mother Nature's pantry of goodies. As for the portable staircase, the answer is, 'of course not.' I'm just putting up a few for show. We'll keep a supply under the cash register to sell."

"We will?"

"Yes. I cleared a spot for them on Friday."

With slackened jaw he contemplated her audacity. Whose deli was this, anyway?

"I don't recall you purchasing shares in my business," he said. "In the future–" Dave, who chose that moment to enter, a white bakery bag in hand, interrupted his lecture.

"Hey–neat! Are those mobiles for sale?"

"Why, yes," Misty answered. She glanced over her shoulder at Gene and wrinkled her nose at him.

"I'll bet Julie, my girlfriend, would like one."

"And I'll bet a cup of coffee you've got doughnuts in that bag," Gene said, coming from behind the counter to set a steaming mug on a nearby table.

"I'm sure she would." Misty held up a mobile in each hand. "Which suits your fancy?"

Dave stepped back to look at both of them. "I'll take the one with the seashell decorations." He sat at the table with the hot brew and opened his bag, selecting a chocolate covered doughnut. "Have you ever dipped a chocolate doughnut in your coffee?" he asked no one in particular. "It sort of makes *café mocha*."

"Somehow, I've missed that pleasure," Gene responded.

Misty slipped the mobile into a plastic bag. Handing the bag to Dave, she said, "This is one of my personal favorites, to. And speaking of seashells, we have fresh crab salad for lunch today."

"That's what smells so good. I'll have a pint to go. And a loaf of that French bread."

Damn, she's good. Shaking his head in resignation, Gene dished up the salad.

Two customers entered–two of the females who routinely flirted outrageously with Gene. They were earlier than usual. Misty turned her attention to them, seating them and quickly providing menus. "Our special today is crab salad," she announced, not wanting them to have an excuse to go to the deli counter and banter with Gene.

Dave finished his coffee and strolled over to Gene. Winking, he said, "That's one bird you should keep firmly in hand."

"She wouldn't stand for having her wings clipped," Gene responded. Then to change the subject, he asked, "What's going on with you and Julie these days?" He handed a bag containing the crab salad and French bread to Dave. "Here's your lunch."

"Thanks. And I just might surprise you with some news on that score."

"Don't tell me Mr. Bachelor-play-the-field is going to pop the question."

Dave grinned and raised his eyebrows. "Yep."

"You think she's ready for marriage?"

"I'll make the offer in such a way she won't be able to refuse." He added, "In fact, you're part of the plan."

"Say again?"

"I want you to do one of your–you know, sexy dinners."

"Surely not in that hole you call an apartment."

"No. This is the special part. We're going out backpacking on Saturday and I want you to deliver the dinner–better make it a late lunch–on Sunday."

Gene laughed. "Now that a novel idea. Didn't think you had it in you. But just how am I supposed to find you two pebbles in the vast foothills?"

"Easy. I'll be sure Julie and I are at the spot where you caught the biggest trout I've ever seen."

Gene scowled, mentally working out details. "You're on if I can get help. I'll call you about the details."

Dave strolled out, whistling *Unforgettable.*

Looking at Misty who was pouring iced tea for a couple of women, Gene inhaled until his lungs protested. He couldn't seem to get her off his mind for a moment.

During the next three hours, Misty sold two more mobiles, each time being sure Gene was aware of the sale.

Over their lunch of crab salad and French bread, Misty's curiosity overcame her reluctance to ask, "Why do you have color labels on so many items?"

His eyes shifted and he directed his gaze to the top of her head. "It's just easier to pick out what I need."

"Then why not use colored lettering instead of the black and white? Or colored paper? I'll re-do the signs for you."

His closed fist came down hard on the table. "No!"

Startled by his booming protest, she grasped the table to steady both it and herself.

He quieted, then massaged the back of his neck. "That is, I like the black on white. It's not gauche, is it?"

Through a disconcerted smile, she said, "Oh, no. Black on white is accepted in the finest of circles."

"Good. Then the signs are just fine the way they are."

She blinked and swallowed. He was concealing something. Something hurtful. She wondered what it was. "The salad's delicious."

"Thanks."

A silence followed, during which time her curiosity again got the better of her. "You like wearing black and white, too, don't you? It's all I've seen you in. Besides blue jeans, of course."

"Yeah. I like black and white." He recalled the times he and his brother, who also had inherited the colorblind gene, had worn different colored socks to school. Humiliated by their peers, and because their mother was too busy with her latest beau to be concerned about them, they engaged their sister to pair their socks. They couldn't trust her, however. When she was mad at one of them, they both had mismatched socks. As an adult, Gene had solved that problem. All of his socks were black.

"Actually," she continued, "with your coloring, you'd look good in earthy colors–yellows, tans, russets, browns." She gazed into his inviting, verdant eyes. "And of course green to match your eyes." Her body temperature rose several degrees. Why can't I just blush in the cheeks like most people, instead of all over she silently grumbled.

He shook his head. "No thanks. I like keeping things simple with black and white. My mind and my closet stay uncluttered."

The door swept open and Lorna whisked her way in. For once, Gene was glad to see her–grateful for the interruption in the conversation. Without waiting for her to look longingly at their food, he rose to prepare a salad.

Smiling broadly, Lorna scooted a chair up to the table and plopped down. Gene placed a plate before her.

"Oh, how sweet of you! I certainly didn't expect lunch."

I'll bet.

"You look like the *Cheshire Cat*, Lorna," Misty remarked. "What's up?"

"Good news, that's what." She took a bite of salad, chewed slowly, then buttered a piece of bread.

Gene thought that Lorna was milking the moment for all the suspense she could squeeze from it. He was gratified that Misty didn't respond by trying to hurry the information out of her roommate. Instead, Misty nonchalantly continued eating. Grinning inwardly, Gene hoped Lorna was frustrated as hell.

"Well, doesn't anyone care what the good news it?" Lorna demanded.

"You've got a new job," Gene said dryly.

"No. I like telling folks how to clean up."

"You won a trip to Hawaii," Misty offered. She glanced at Gene and he winked encouragingly.

Lorna released a thwarted sigh. "No. It's not about me. Not really, anyway." She looked at Misty. "It's about you." She hesitated, heightening expectation. "Raymond asked me to show him the Victorian house you want." She glanced dreamily toward the ceiling.

Misty sat straighter in her chair. "Go on."

"He can be quite charming and persuasive. He convinced me I'd be doing it for your best interests, Misty, so I took him to where it is."

Misty's chest felt suddenly tight. She could manage only a shallow intake of breath. "I told him to forget that evening ever happened. That included asking him for a loan."

"But he might just buy the house and offer to rent it to you. He made me promise not to tell you, but after all, you are my roommate, and I know he'll never find out because you won't tell him I broke my promise."

Pensive, Misty didn't respond.

"You won't tell him, will you?" demanded Lorna.

Misty stared at her plate, making idle circles with her fork. "No, of course not." The Victorian house was what she wanted, wasn't it? She could set up her own business and be her own boss. It was the answer to her prayers, wasn't it? So why did she now feel ambivalent about it–not about owning her own business, but about having the home virtually given to her? She didn't want to be indebted to anyone. But it was more than that. She wanted to make it on her own.

On the other hand, Gene was on her mind far, far too much. He was with her when she taught her class. He was with her when she bathed. And she willed him to be with her when she was in bed. She shook her head. She needed to be away from him.

With furrowed brow, Gene stared at Misty and waited impatiently for her to respond. He willed her not to accept the offer from the scumbag.

"Well, my goodness," Lorna said. "Here I come with such terrific news and you act like you couldn't care less."

"I appreciate your coming, Lorna. Honestly. I was just thinking is all."

"How about some tea, ladies?" Gene offered.

"Not for me. The lunch was delicious, but I have to run." Lorna smiled at Gene, and saucily tilted her head to the side. "Thanks ever so much." She leapt up from the table, took several hurried steps, then slowed to a saunter, swinging her hips as if she were doing a hula. She glanced over her shoulder at Gene and bumped into the door jam.

"Your hip okay?" Gene asked.

Flustered, Lorna quickly opened the door and vanished.

A pregnant silence followed. Gene finally broke it. "I thought you weren't going to give Raymond the time of day."

Still regarding her plate, Misty responded, "He showed up at my apartment full of apologies. And after all, I'm not totally blameless for the disastrous evening."

Why was she explaining this to him? Yet she continued: "For our families' sakes, I felt we needed to resolve the issue."

He nodded, his mouth firm. "Looks like it was worth it. Apparently you'll have your business handed to you on a silver platter."

His sarcasm rankled her. She looked him squarely in the eye. "Apparently so."

He stood to clear the table, rattling the mugs until Misty feared he'd break them. He's just concerned about the possibility of losing a good employee, she reasoned.

Gene marched behind the counter. *Why the hell should I care what she does? Because you like her, dunderhead. And you don't want her accepting anything from that dirt bag.*

Preparing to leave for the day, Misty removed her apron and picked up her purse while avoiding eye contact with Gene. She started for the door when he called her name. She halted in mid-stride. Without turning, she responded, "Yes?"

He wished he didn't need her help the following Sunday. He didn't want to be with her for a whole day. But the fact was, he did need help. He was contracted for Dave's dinner and he couldn't do by himself. "Want to make up for the two non-dinner dinners?"

Wary, she slowly turned and asked, "What did you have in mind?"

"Another *Dinner for Two* on Sunday."

"If I were you, I wouldn't trust me not to ruin it."

"Third time's the charm."

She owed it to him. "All right. I'll do it."

"This dinner's more like a late lunch, so we have to leave in the morning."

Her interest piqued, she asked, "Where exactly will we be going?"

Ignoring her question, he stacked the dishes in the dishwasher. "Have you ever done any backpacking?"

"No overnight trips. Just hiking with a daypack. Why?"

"That'll do. We'll be hiking down Miners' Ravine to Gold River."

She knew that was in the foothills of the Sierra, but couldn't place the exact spot. "And hauling all the equipment necessary for a gourmet dinner?"

"Yep. Except the table. We'll serve the happy couple on the ground. On a lace tablecloth, of course."

"Of course. Now would you tell me what this is all about?"

"Dave just asked me to do it. He wants to propose to Julie in a unique, mushy way, and thought a *Dinner For Two* in the wilds would fill the bill."

Misty smiled, although she didn't like Gene's derogatory use of the word "mushy." "That's a marvelous idea! Very romantic. Don't you think so?"

He shrugged. "I guess."

For a man who makes a tidy profit on cozy dinners for two he has little romance in his soul.

Bent at the waist, Lorna tilted her head toward the floor and vigorously brushed her hair. "Now remember to act surprised when Raymond shows up this evening."

"Don't worry. I'm working on raising my eyebrows." Misty inspected her fingernails, evaluating her filing job. She rounded the last nail, then buffed all ten. "Working with dried materials plays havoc with a manicure."

"I'll scoot out of here," Lorna said, "so you and Raymond can be alone."

"Oh, no you won't. If you leave, I leave." Misty didn't want to face Raymond at all, but being alone with him was unthinkable. How would she tell him she didn't want the Victorian home? Could she do it and still maintain a semblance of friendship?

"If you insist."

Misty glanced sharply at her roommate. "You're usually not that easy to convince. But then, the last time I saw you with Raymond, you were mirroring his movements."

"Well, after all, I felt kinda sorry for him. I mean–"

"Yes, I know," Misty interrupted. "Raymond was no longer a rapist, but an unfortunate, deceived man."

"He certainly was." Lorna straightened, flipping her hair to her back. She slid a wide red hair band in place.

Misty suppressed a grin. "Weren't you just telling me that red is the color that most attracts men?"

Lorna's cheeks flashed bright pink. "Was I? I don't recall."

"You'd better decide if you want Raymond or Gene. You can't have them both."

"Gene is a lost cause," Lorna said, adjusting her hair band. "He's nuts about you."

"You have a vivid imagination. He's only *nuts* about his business." Yet, a pleasurable wave broke over her at the thought of Gene caring for her as a woman, not as a valued employee.

The doorbell rang. Misty shivered. Mustering courage, she sauntered to the door and managed to feign appropriate surprise at seeing Raymond across the threshold. They exchanged pleasantries and she invited him into the living room.

Lorna emerged from her bedroom wearing a tee shirt that matched her headband. "I made an angel food cake today, Raymond. It's low in calories and has absolutely no cholesterol. Would you care for some?"

"Icing?" he inquired.

"No icing."

"In that case, I'll have a piece."

"Coming right up," Lorna sang as she waltzed to the kitchen.

Misty wanted to gag. She also wanted to get the confrontation over with. "What brings you here this evening, Raymond?"

"Can't a man visit an old friend?"

"Yes, of course. It's just that you've never popped in like this before."

"As a matter of fact, I do have another reason for coming." He paused, smirking. "I have quite a surprise for you. I'm negotiating to purchase the Victorian you had your eye on."

Misty started to speak, but Raymond interrupted.

"I quite agree that it's in a prime location for a small

business and when negotiations are complete, I'll be prepared to rent it to you."

Lorna entered carrying a tray with a teapot, cups, and three servings of angel food cake. "Here we are," she hummed.

Raymond smiled at her. "Sweet of you."

Lorna pursed her lips. "Sweets for the sweet."

Trying to ignore the sparks between the two, Misty said, "I appreciate what you're trying to do, Raymond, but I've changed my mind."

Tea sloshed out of the pot as Lorna sat the tray down hard on the coffee table.

"Changed your mind? But I've practically purchased the damn thing," Raymond exclaimed.

Misty couldn't explain why she felt close to tears. "I'm sorry, Raymond, but you really should have talked with me about it first."

"But–" he sputtered.

"I really can't discuss it further." Misty rose, raced to her bedroom, and closed the door. Shaking, she sat unsteadily on her bed. No, she didn't want to be in Raymond's debt. Not in anyone's debt. When she started a business, it would be the result of her own sweat and tears. The Victorian house she had her heart set on wouldn't be available then, but something else would come along.

An ache in her heart reminded her that when she had her own business, she wouldn't be with Gene any longer.

Driving east on Interstate 80, Gene announced, "The

next exit, Gold Run, is ours." He curved off the freeway. A sign to the right read: "Argonaut Ravine Road–Two Miles." A sign to the left read: "Miners' Ravine Road–One Mile." He turned left.

"Hope you don't mind mountain roads," Gene said.

"Not at all."

"Good, 'cause this one's a doozie."

"Ah...exactly how do you mean that?"

"From Miners' Ravine, it's a snake-like dirt road up to the trailhead. Elevation increases fast and steady." Noting that she tensed, he quickly added, "But it's only eight miles."

She guessed she could put up with any kind of road for that distance.

On the other hand, she hadn't counted on this road. One way with hairpin turns most of the eight miles, it hugged the mountain on one side and was sheer, steep granite on the other, sans guardrail. Misty grasped either side of her seat and, wide-eyed, looked straight ahead.

Swinging from curve to curve, Gene said, "Feels a little like downhill skiing, only uphill, don't you think?"

"Oh, sure," a white-knuckled Misty responded. She didn't relax until half an hour later when they reached the road's end.

"That's Dave's car." Gene indicated the lone car, a sporty red Miata, parked at the trailhead.

Misty stepped out of the car and inhaled deeply, greedily, of the heavily laden, pine-scented air.

Gene unloaded the gear and helped Misty strap on a backpack. "It won't be as heavy coming back up."

That's a blessing, she thought with a silent moan. Why hadn't she asked more questions before agreeing to this adventure? Or, rather, misadventure. *Because you want to be alone with Gene.* She dismissed that thought. "What kind of trail is it we'll be hiking?"

"Switchbacks all the way down to the river. It'll take us about an hour."

She remembered switchbacks from day hiking, those sharp turns that make going downhill easier. However, it took her a minute to digest fully his last piece of information. Incredulous, she asked, "An hour down. So that means two hours back up?"

He shrugged into his backpack. "About that."

Well, if Dave's girlfriend can do it, Misty reasoned, so can I. *Damn. Why didn't I join that fitness center?*

"Let's go," he said, stepping out.

Why, he's anxious to do this, Misty realized. He looks like a kid staring at unopened birthday presents. She quickened her step to stay abreast of him.

"What are you fixing for dinner?"

"Steak Diane. I took the steaks out of the freezer just before we left, so they'll be about right when we get there." He gazed with amusement at her ponytail that swayed from side to side, keeping time with her steps. She was a good sport to agree to help with this rather unusual dinner, he thought.

As they descended the rocky switchbacks, Misty was pleased with the deftness of her steps. At one point she stopped to peer straight down the side of the mountain. Looking at the slippery granite, she said, "Looks like it'd be easier to slide down than walk the rest of the way."

Gene's brows furrowed. "I hope you're kidding. That'd be dangerous as hell."

The lower the pair descended, the less menacing the side of the mountain became. As they rounded one switchback, they spotted a herd of deer grazing in a velvet green meadow some hundred feet off the side of the trail. Gene smiled at Misty's awe over the beauty of the scene. The meadow, sprinkled and puddled with wildflowers, was ringed with evergreens.

Breathless, Misty asked, "Have you ever seen such colorful beauty?"

"Ah, no," he honestly replied.

Speaking softly, Gene said, "Let's watch the deer a while."

Quietly, they moved to a large boulder where they sat, hip to hip, drinking in the scene before them. They counted eight deer. Tuning into the sounds around her, Misty realized they were surrounded by wildlife. She heard, then saw, two woodpeckers energetically gathering brunch on the trunk of a pine tree.

"I feel like Snow White in the woods with all these animals about me," she whispered. *And you'd be a majestic Prince Charming.* She pictured her companion in a regal outfit atop a white steed.

"I hate to leave this scenic banquet," Gene said, "but we'd better go." He took her hand to help her up, holding it in his a bit longer than absolutely necessary.

After descending a few more switchbacks, they were able to see the river, then a few more after that and they were on the bottom of the canyon.

"Now how do we find your friends?" Misty asked.

"I know exactly where they are. Dave and I planned a rendezvous point. We've hiked all over this canyon together. See that log across the river?" He pointed about a quarter of a mile downstream.

Misty nodded.

"We'll cross there."

"We will?"

"No problem. You've got good boots on and I'll help you."

Misty worried, remembering that she had spent her entire childhood with scabby knees. She was always falling on them. She could easily fall into the river and ruin another dinner. Worse, she'd look like a fool in front of Gene. Her mouth suddenly dry, she resisted the urge to take off her pack and clamor back up the trail. Instead, she kept in step with Gene, smiling weakly and pretending that she was used to such shenanigans on a daily basis.

When they reached the log, Gene hopped up and extended a hand to Misty. She grabbed hold and held fast.

"Just look straight ahead," Gene directed, "not down at the river."

A sudden calm enveloped her. As long as she held his massive hand and followed his footsteps, she knew she'd be all right. When they reached the other side, she felt giddy with pleasure and confidence over accomplishing the feat with ease.

They delved deeper into the woods until Gene came to an abrupt halt. Turning to Misty, he said, "Be very quiet now. Dave doesn't want Julie to know about this until we suddenly appear with appetizers and champagne."

"They're near here?" Misty whispered.

"Just around the next boulder."

Misty sniffed and detected a whiff of smoke from a campfire.

Gene shrugged off his backpack and helped Misty with hers. He slid it off, down over her derriere that so nicely filled out her jeans.

She watched while he carefully removed each item, admiring his efficiency and resourcefulness. "You brought just the exact amount of each ingredient you'd need?" she asked.

"Right. Why pack what I won't use?"

Some of the food was surrounded by ice, accounting for part of the weight they wouldn't have to haul up the switchbacks. Also, she realized, an empty champagne bottle is lighter than a full one.

Gene arranged the hors d'oeuvres on a small crystal platter. "You take these," he directed. "I'll get the champagne and glasses."

Misty accepted the relish tray and picked up two linen napkins.

"We're ready," Gene said. "Now give that dinner bell a ring."

"I thought you didn't want to warn them."

"Well, just in case...I mean, you never know what

they might be doing."

"Oh." Misty's body warmed several degrees.

She jiggled the silver bell, which emitted high-pitched musical notes, then followed Gene, weaving through manzanita bushes and around a huge boulder.

The couple was stretched out on a double sleeping bag...reading. Misty was relieved.

"*Dinner for Two,*" Gene announced.

Julie sat straight up. "Gene!" Then she turned to a grinning Dave and threw her arms around his neck.

The pair looked enough alike to be brother and sister, Misty noted. Both were small-boned with short curly hair and brown eyes. Julie had a sprinkle of freckles across her nose.

Gene made introductions.

Julie smiled and nodded. "I might have known you had planned something like this when you insisted you'd take care of this evening's meal," she said to Dave. She turned to Misty. "He can't cook anything."

"That's not true," Dave protested. "I grill a mean hamburger."

"I also wondered why you wanted to start a campfire so early," Julie said.

After plying the couple with appetizers and champagne, Gene and Misty disappeared back to their packs.

"They look so happy." Misty sighed, pin pricks of envy jabbing at her.

"Uh-huh," Gene mumbled. He prepared the salad and arranged it on individual plates. Misty took the lace tablecloth, returned to the couple, and placed it on the sleeping bag. Then she set out napkins, silverware, and candleholders. The obvious delight that Dave's and Julie's faces registered warmed and pleased her, making her tasks joyful.

Gene served the salad then prepared the steak Diane over the campfire, making a performance of his culinary expertise. First, he browned the pounded steaks in butter. With a flourish, he poured brandy over the meat. Julie gasped with pleasure when he set the brandy aflame. When the flaming stopped, he added chalets and chives, sautéed them, then added the final ingredient, dry sherry.

Misty, sharing the campfire, warmed tiny red potatoes in butter then sprinkled them with minced parsley. Her stomach growled.

Julie inhaled audibly. "I must be dreaming. This couldn't be a campfire dinner I'm smelling!"

"Even beats doughnuts," Dave added.

When the main dish was served, Gene set the silver dinner bell beside the couple. "Ring when you're ready for dessert," he directed. He walked toward the boulder, Misty close on his heels.

"This is so delightful–the outdoors, the trees, the animals, the walk and the dinner. Thanks for asking me to help."

"Hope you'll still feel that way while you're trudging back up the trail." He rounded the boulder than turned to face her. A smile on his lips, he lightly grasped her shoulders. "You'd make a terrific Girl Scout."

Speechless, she lost herself in the cool green of his

eyes.

Gene's voice box malfunctioned. More than anything he'd ever know, he wanted to kiss her. Instead, he said, "We both act like we're starving. No wonder. It's way past lunch time." He hunkered down on his haunches to rummage through his pack. "Sorry, but we don't get steak Diane or a lace tablecloth." He handed Misty a deli sandwich. "Pull up a boulder, have a seat, and feast on this."

She sat on the ground, leaned against a boulder, and munched. "Turkey and Swiss cheese. It's great."

Gene washed his sandwich down with a Coke. "Want to see the dessert?" he asked.

"You did a cake?"

"Uh-huh. Coincidence that you mentioned Snow White today."

Carefully, he opened a box lined with reusable freezer packs, then gently lifted out a small, round plastic dome-lidded cake. He removed the cover.

"Whew," he said, relieved. "The icing is intact."

A miniature Snow White, one arm gracefully outstretched, looked demurely at Prince Charming who was holding and kissing the proffered hand. Birds circled their heads and a spotted fawn stood next them.

"It's darling," Misty said. "It should be a music box. Why, Dave and Julie will be thrilled."

"Mushy enough?" he asked.

She stiffened. "If you mean is it romantic? Yes, it is."

The silver bell tinkled.

"Good. Let's serve it then leave them alone."

Misty's body heated at the thought of what they'd be doing when left alone.

When Julie saw the cake, she scrambled for her camera, snapping several pictures at different angles.

Gene and Misty left them with a cake knife and freshly perked coffee.

"Does Dave have a ring with him?" Misty asked as they packed their gear. "Does he plan on proposing before or after dessert?"

Gene shrugged. "What's the difference just so long as it gets done?"

Her lips thinned with vexation. Why didn't he see that the proposal itself was the most important part of the celebration? The rest was foreplay. She stifled a giggle at her metaphor.

Packs lighter, they struck out. When they reached the log, Gene offered his hand, but Misty confidently refused, and was pleased with how easily she crossed.

Hiking up the switchbacks wasn't as bad as Misty had envisioned. I must be in better shape than I thought, she mused.

On the drive home, Gene said, "Since this was such a breeze for you, how about helping me a week from Sunday?"

"Tell me what you have in mind."

"Dinner in the bay area."

Arlene Evans

Chapter 5

Gene parked his van along the waterfront in Sausalito. A few snowy clouds powdered an otherwise clear blue sky, a perfect covering for the pleasure sailing crafts, some moored, others gliding in the San Francisco Bay. He deeply inhaled the salted air.

He gazed silently for a few moments at the ethereal scene, then said, "Let's take a walk."

Turning in her seat, Misty glanced at his rugged profile, as pleased by the sight of his handsome face as by the serene scene on the bay. "I though we needed to leave early to give you extra time to prepare for the dinner which somehow turned out to be a brunch," she said, perplexed.

He shook his head. "What we have here is a classic example of a failure to communicate." Misty noted that he didn't have eye contact with her when he spoke–rather, he continued looking at the sailboats. "Actually, I needed to have time to stroll before the dinner. There's something relaxing about seeing those little white triangles floating out on the bay."

Misty gazed at the sailing crafts. "It is a lovely picture. But why didn't you tell me you needed to do this?" she asked, mystified by his use of the word *needed.*

He turned to face her. "Because you might have thought that was too chummy a thing to do with the boss and said 'No.'" He opened the car door, slid out, then went around to the passenger side, and opened her door.

She considered that she wouldn't have refused. *Heaven help her, she wanted to be with him.* Thankful her feelings weren't obvious to him, she folded her arms on her chest and said, "You tricked me."

"Yeah," he agreed. He gently grasped her arm. "Let's go."

She allowed herself to be extracted from the vehicle, then fell in step beside him.

"Now what was it you said about brunch instead of dinner?" she asked.

"Not instead of. In addition to."

She halted in mid-stride and turned to face him. Momentarily, she was distracted by the sight of the sun striking his russet hair, breaking, then sending miniscule shards of light in every direction. She blinked back to the situation at hand. "Now suppose you tell me the whole truth, and nothing but the truth. From the top."

She's trying her damnedest to look irritated, he thought. He could see the longing in her eyes. *Hell, he could skip brunch and just feast on the sight of her.* But that wasn't the reason he asked her to come with him today. After today she'd run the other way. That wasn't the way he wanted it, but that's the way it needed to be.

He took her arm and guided her into a stroll. "Brunch is at the Charthouse." He had chosen the Charthouse because he wanted the meal and the ambience to be memorable.

"The Charthouse."

"You'll love it. Trust me."

"You've not made yourself very trustworthy."

"It has a great view of San Francisco and the Bay."

"You're changing the subject. You're telling me that you're not preparing brunch."

"Of course not. I'm preparing dinner. The ingredients are all in the coolers in the van."

"Now let me guess the rest. You didn't tell me we were having brunch together because you thought I might refuse."

"Exactly."

Wrong again.

Unable to resist the urge, Gene slipped an arm around her shoulders. Almost immediately, he felt her arm around his waist. *Lord help me she does want me*, he thought.

Being close to Gene, their arms about each other, enhanced the pleasure Misty felt strolling in this quiet, elegant, Mediterranean-like village.

"Here we are," Gene said. "The Charthouse." He swung the door open allowing delicious aromas to waft through.

The combination of the aromas, the picturesque dining room, and the man she was with brought a smile of infinite pleasure to Misty's lips.

A server escorted them to a table for two by an expansive window. Reluctantly, they released each other. The server held Misty's chair, scooted her in, then opened a menu for each of them. Misty scanned the vast array of food choices. Fortunately, she thought, she hadn't eaten breakfast. "What would you recommend?"

"The Eggs Benedict are...." He lowered his voice and leaned toward her. "Almost as good as those I make."

She chuckled. "I'll try them. My mother used to make them every Sunday, but I haven't had them for ages."

The waiter appeared and Gene placed the order.

"Tell me about your mother."

"She's a professional homemaker and volunteer to the world. My parents were married fourteen years before I came along. They're retired now, living in Arizona. We keep in close touch."

"You're an only child?"

"Yes. I often wondered what it would be like to have siblings. I envied my friends who had brothers and sisters. How about you? Any sisters or brothers?"

"One of each. We fought a lot."

His answer was brusque, as if he wanted to close the subject. She didn't pursue it.

"After brunch, will we have time to go through the boutiques?" she asked.

Gene tried not to frown. Browsing in those little specialty stores along the waterfront wasn't his favorite activity. "Boutiques?"

"Yes." She perceived with relish his discomfiture. "And the galleries."

Now the galleries he could tolerate. "We have some time," he conceded.

Her dark eyes flashed with amusement. "You're being cooperative in order to compensate for tricking me into coming," she challenged.

"Could be." He felt grateful she wasn't angry with him for not telling the whole truth.

For two hours after brunch Gene trailed a meandering Misty through the array of boutiques and galleries, often admiring her planes and curves rather than the displayed merchandise or artwork. He particularly liked following her up the various stairways.

A glass miniature of Snow White caught Gene's eye. He purchased it and gave it to Misty.

Delighted, Misty held the statue at arm's length to catch the light. "It's lovely." She turned to face Gene. "Thank you–" She stopped speaking when he sighed audibly, his mouth down-turned.

"Guess we'd better go," he said.

She had a disturbing urge to nibble at his down-turned lip.

"I don't understand. If you didn't want to do this job, why did you accept it?"

"It's for my mother."

"Your mother?" He wants me to meet his mother! She tried to remain calm at the possible implication of this revelation.

"Yes. And her new husband. The sixth, I think. Although it could be her seventh. I've lost count. I lost count of her boyfriends years ago. They're just a blur."

Misty detected anger and resentment in Gene's voice. Did she also hear resignation, like an old familiar wound recently reopened? She remembered her own parents, of their long, loving marriage and of the intimacy she felt with both her mother and her father. She couldn't relate, couldn't empathize with estrangement from one's parents. She didn't know how to respond to him, what anesthetic to use to dull his pain.

"You said there'd be four for dinner. Who are the other two?"

"You and me."

Silently, Misty turned and headed toward the van.

"What, no anger? No accusations of concealing the truth?" Gene almost wished she would get angry. Her silent withdrawal was almost more than he could tolerate. He caught up with her and placed his left arm lightly around her shoulders, fearing she'd shake it off. "I really do need your help. For more than just serving the dinner. I don't know how I can get through another evening with yet another new step-father."

"Just tell me now if there are any more little surprises."

Like a magician on stage, he raised his right hand to show an empty palm. "None. Not that I know of anyway. I haven't met this new husband myself. You'll be greeting number six–or seven–right along with me."

She considered this. "So you want me to be a buffer

between you and your mother and her new husband."

"No, not really. I wouldn't put you in that position. I thought your presence would temper my opinion of my mother and help me view her more objectively." *Besides, you're good company and nice to look at.*

Befuddled by her feelings, Misty wanted to put her arms around his broad shoulders, to comfort him and tell him everything would be okay. That's what he'd do for her, she reasoned, but at that moment she felt she couldn't penetrate the shell of cynicism he'd erected around himself.

They reached the van and silently slid in. A ten-minute drive took them into the hills of the East Bay. Garden walls of stucco or brick surrounded many of the elegant homes, affording only a glimpse of manicured gardens.

"The people living in these mansions obviously have regular gardening services," Misty observed.

"And housekeeping services," Gene added.

"Your mother lives here?"

He nodded.

"She must be…well-heeled."

"Her second husband was wealthy. He died and left her a bundle."

"And your father?"

He didn't respond.

"I'm sorry." Misty dropped her gaze to an annoying hangnail. "I didn't mean to pry."

He arched, then evened his eyebrows. "My father left the fold shortly after my sister was born. He hasn't been seen or heard from since. We lived in poverty until my mother re-married."

Gene nosed the van into a circular driveway and brought it to a stop in front of a home that could have provided the cover story for *House Beautiful.* A half-acre of perfectly buzzed deep green lawn led to the two-story white Colonial. Native coastal live oaks surrounded the house providing veiled seclusion. Tree ferns abounded amidst orderly bursts of color provided by rhododendrons, fuchsias, and day lilies.

"Gorgeous," Misty breathed. "Have you ever seen such lovely colors?"

"Uh, no," Gene replied honestly. "But the aroma of the trees and grass is delicious. Let's get this stuff unpacked."

They each removed an ice chest from the back of the van and walked up the marble stairs to the landing. Gene shifted the chest under one arm and knocked.

A tall, slender, coppery-haired woman answered the door. Her eyes were a fading version of Gene's, her cheekbones high and her features angled. Dressed in a shimmering green silk shift that brushed her shoulders and hips, she exuded an aura of stately sophistication.

Misty felt suddenly drab in her "uniform" of black slacks and white blouse. In order to look plain, she had coiled her hair into a bun and applied no makeup except lip-gloss. But those efforts were superfluous–Gene's mother could make any woman look plain.

On closer inspection, Misty realized that, although russet may have been the color of the woman's hair at one time, her perfectly even color tone came from a drug store bottle. Or more likely from a high-priced beautician's magic. Misty considered the chunky bracelets and the pear-shaped diamonds dangling from the woman's earlobes a bit heavy for the dress.

"Darling!" the woman enthused. She stretched her arms and bent over the ice chest Gene carried to hug him, then kiss him on the cheek.

Gene teetered back. "June–this Misty Jones."

Misty had heard of people who called their parents by their first names, but she had never actually known one who did until now.

"Misty, this is my mother June…June…"

"Shepherd, silly. My last name's Shepherd."

Today.

She widened the door. "Come in, my dears." Seizing one handle of Misty's cooler, she said, "Let me help you with that." She led the way to the kitchen and assisted Misty in lifting the chest to a massive wooden counter. "Misty and Jones. I like that combination. Did your father name you?" She wrapped an arm around Misty's waist and squeezed.

Misty's initial impression of an imposing, sophisticated lady evaporated.

"Yes. How did you know?"

Gracefully, she waved a multi-braceleted arm in the air. "It's charmingly like a man to take a salt-of-the-earth name like Jones and spice it up with a unique moniker like Misty."

Suddenly relaxed in June's presence, Misty smiled.

"That's exactly what he had in mind," she confirmed.

"Now come along to the garden you two and meet Hector."

Gene grimaced. "Hector?"

"Yes. He's from an old San Francisco family." She shielded her mouth with her hand and quietly added, "He's loaded." With an arm hooked around Misty's elbow, she led the way through the patio door to the garden, where a tall, flabby sixty-something Hector was breathing audibly while stooping to trim rosebushes.

"Hector, darling, meet the prodigal son, Gene, and his lovely lady, Misty."

Misty felt her mercury rise. His lady? Just what had Gene told his mother about their relationship?

Hector extended his hand to Gene who accepted and shook it. "Sorry you couldn't have made it to the wedding. Your sister and brother were there." He removed his visor and wiped his forehead with his sleeve.

"And how are my sibs?" Gene asked.

June raised her arms in a helpless gesture. "Searching for new mates, the poor dears."

Gene glanced at Misty for signs of shock, but found only interest on her countenance.

"You know, darling," June continued, "You really should make more of an effort to take part in family gatherings."

If he went to all the weddings in this family, Gene thought, he wouldn't have time for anything else.

"Been pretty busy getting the new business off the ground," Gene hedged. "Don't have much spare time."

"If you had accepted my offer to finance your charming venture you'd have a much easier time of it. The offer is still viable, darling."

"Thanks, June, but I'd rather do it on my own."

Misty's lips firmed and her eyes narrowed. He had an ulterior motive for inviting me, she concluded. He's making it on his own and feels I should do the same. *Mr. Virtuous.* Well, she was glad she hadn't told him she'd refused Raymond's offer. It was none of his business. She wouldn't tell him if he tortured her.

Gene excused himself to go to the kitchen to commence dinner preparations.

With her interest in flowers, Misty had no difficulty keeping up an animated conversation with Hector and June. Later, she followed Gene's directions to set up and serve the dinner, but said only what was absolutely necessary to him. During dinner she ate only half of her Lobster Thermadore while continuing to chat about flowers and gardens with the newlyweds.

Gene pretended not to notice Misty's coldness toward him. She understands my background now, he thought. My inheritance. She wants nothing more to do with me, and for good reason. He continued the visit for what he considered an acceptable length of time, then murmured excuses and packed to leave. With promises to return soon, he steered Misty to the van to make his getaway.

As he maneuvered the car out of the driveway, Misty asked, "Just what did you tell your mother about our relationship?"

"Nothing. Why?"

"I got the impression she thought we were living together."

"Not surprising if you knew June. She thinks that if a man and woman aren't living together, they should be. My brother and sister are between second and third marriages–or maybe it's third and fourth–but you can bet they're not living alone." He couldn't make his family situation any plainer than that.

She bit her lower lip. "Okay. But you wanted me to know that your mother offered to finance your business, didn't you?"

"Huh?"

"You're making it on your own and you think I should refuse Raymond's offer." Momentarily, she wondered if this was the real reason she felt irritated with Gene or was she just using it as an excuse? She found it difficult to admit, but she was uneasy, even a little frightened, by her growing attraction to him.

This wasn't going as he'd planned. She seemed totally unruffled by all the marital disunity in his family, but upset by some silly remark his mother had made.

"Now that you've brought it up, what are you going to do about Raymond's offer?"

"That's really none of your business, is it?"

Glowering, he said, "It is if I need to find new help."

Shocked and hurt, she responded, "Oh. I see." She swallowed hard. "That's what's really worrying you. You might lose your help. Well, to cut the suspense, consider this my two weeks' notice."

Gene slipped the HELP WANTED sign in the deli window. Even if she did give me the cold shoulder for the wrong reason, it's just as well, he thought. With their affinity for each other, they were headed for a chapel as sure as night follows day, and that's something they might both regret. Considering his family trait of disastrous marriages, the likelihood of him having a permanent relationship was remote at best.

Gene started to turn from the window when a floral delivery van pulled up to the curb in front of the deli, drawing his attention back to the street. A teenager leapt out of the van and bounced up to the door, bouquet in hand. Gene opened the door.

"Does Misty Jones work here?" the petite brunette inquired.

Gene nodded. He couldn't figure out why women got so excited about receiving flowers. Roses are red, he'd learned, and leaves are green, but the bouquet of buds and lacy trims could all have been dirt brown as far as he was concerned. He could appreciate the form, texture, and scent, but otherwise, roses were strictly blah.

"Is she here?" the girl asked in a squeaky voice.

"No, but you can leave them on the counter. She'll be here later." He hoped she'd be here later. She'd been in such a snit when he left her the night before that she may have changed her mind about giving two weeks' notice.

Lunch business was brisker every day and he definitely needed her help. He dreaded the thought of training someone new, but maybe the greater dread was the thought of never seeing Misty again. He pictured her sparkle as she tended the customers, a ready smile charming both males and females. He sighed.

The delivery girl set the vase on the counter, stepped back to observe the position, then moved forward to rotate the vase to the left. "Be sure to add water," she instructed as the door closed behind her.

"Yeah, sure," he said to the empty room. Frowning, Gene assumed the flowers were from that scumbag Raymond, congratulating Misty on her new business and nudging her closer to his expensive bedroom. And he was rubbing Gene's nose in it by sending the roses to the deli.

Gene managed to raise leaden feet to get himself behind the counter to prepare Oysters Rockefeller.

He didn't look up when Misty entered; but he was surprised by the deep breath he needed to pull in when he sensed her presence. In his peripheral vision he could see that her hair was brushed off her creamy cheeks, a black velvet band holding it in place. Damn but she looked good. He wondered how she felt seeing the HELP WANTED sign in the window. Relieved, he assumed. Now she was free to pursue her own career. To take Raymond up on his offer.

Misty stepped in front of the floral display. "Roses from Mrs. Anderson?" she queried. "All is forgiven?"

Gene grunted, not at all amused by her sarcasm.

Stepping closer to the roses to check the card, she exclaimed in mock surprise, "Oh, they're for me!"

He blinked and glanced in her direction. He wondered what she'd do if he went to her, masterfully grasped her shoulders, pulled her to him, and took possession of her sexy mouth. He shrugged. *She'd probably just tell me I smelled like oysters.*

He watched while she slipped the card out of the small envelope. She stared at it as if trying to comprehend the message. Did he read disappointment in her expression? No, that must be his imagination. All women loved roses. She stuffed the card in her pants pocket.

"I don't want those flowers in here stinking up the place," Gene grumbled. "They clash with the oysters."

Misty swept the vase off the counter, her face waxen. "I'll put them in our unisex bathroom."

Our bathroom? Maybe she hadn't emotionally broken from the deli. He shook his head, disgusted with himself for his wishful thinking.

He considered reminding her to put water in the vase, but dismissed the notion. He hoped the roses rotted by that afternoon. He forced his attention back to the oysters.

A steady stream of customers kept Gene and Misty busy through the lunch hour. The last two customers, seated in a corner table, lingered over their oysters, engrossed in conversation. They were tall, slender men in dark business suits whom Gene had seen on several other occasions. He wondered if they'd continue coming in after Misty was gone. Simultaneously, they rose and approached Gene.

The younger of the two men spoke: "We certainly enjoy the seafood dishes you've been preparing lately."

Nodding his appreciation, Gene said, "Thanks. Glad to hear it."

The older man cleared his throat. "Do you do catering?"

"Certainly."

"Could you do a seafood dinner combining all the dishes you've prepared lately?" The younger one again this time. They were taking turns speaking. Gene felt like a spectator at a tennis match, his head bobbing back and forth.

"Sure could." He looked at the older man, knowing it was his turn to talk.

"For three hundred people?"

Gene gulped. He'd never prepared a dinner for more than eight.

"It's a political fund raiser," the younger one explained, "with all the big names. Everything has to be perfect."

Gene nodded, beads of sweat popping out on his forehead. "I understand."

"Do you have a regular crew that works for you?" inquired the older.

"*Uhh…*" Gene hedged.

"Oh, yes. A regular crew," Misty interjected.

Where the hell does she come off, speaking for me? Gene opened his mouth to protest, but was interrupted.

"Good," said the younger. "We can't afford any more mishaps. We had to discharge the original caterer we hired and change locations."

"You'll find us more than dependable," Misty assured

both men, her smile captivating them. "Would you like clam chowder and a green salad to compliment the dinner?"

The men glanced at each other and nodded approvingly.

"And of course we'll order French bread direct from Fisherman's Wharf," she added.

The hell we will, thought Gene. I ought to shake some sense into her.

"Where is the banquet to be held?" Misty continued brightly.

The two men looked at each other as if they had forgotten whose turn it was to speak. They regained their composure and the elder replied, "In the annex of the Senator Lounge."

"Excellent choice," Misty said.

Gene shook his head, bewildered by her effrontery.

"In a month," the younger added. "The twenty-first of next month to be exact. Can you handle it then?"

"Let me see. The twenty-first, you say." She walked behind the counter, opened a drawer, and rustled some papers. With a self-assured nod, Misty replied, "Lucky. The twenty-first is open."

Gene's mouth went suddenly dry. He couldn't swallow, much less speak. He smiled weakly.

"Good," both men responded. The younger nodded to the older who added, "Including wine, we were thinking in the neighborhood of thirty-five dollars per person. Does that sound reasonable to you?"

"Well," Misty hedged, "that's a rather poor

neighborhood. We'll discuss exactly what we can prepare for thirty-five dollars, including wine."

Brow furrowed, the younger said, "Thirty-seven fifty is absolute tops. Will it be convenient for you if we return tomorrow with a contract?"

Gene's jaw gaped. "Uh…" he squeaked.

"Tomorrow would be most convenient," Misty replied.

The men nodded in unison and briskly left the deli.

"Are you crazy?" Gene blurted. "Where do you get off with your, 'A green salad and clam chowder will compliment the dinner,' and 'We'll order French bread from Fisherman's Wharf'?" He batted his lashes and did his best to imitate her smile.

Hands on hips, Misty squared her shoulders and straightened her spine. "Well, my remarks were certainly preferable to standing transfixed like an open-mouthed sphinx!"

"Who could get a word in edgewise with your incessant chatter? Do you realize I've never done any kind of banquet? I don't have the least idea how to go about organizing one."

"Well, I have, and I do. In the Peace Corps I often organized dinners for three hundred or more."

"Gourmet dinners?"

"Well, no…"

"You're talking about soup kitchen dinners, aren't you?"

"Well, they were served family style," she said. "And they took a great deal of organization. I also did a wedding reception once."

He groaned. "Swell. Ideal experience."

She skewed her mouth in a gesture of disgust as if to dismiss his protest. "How about a little optimism here? And a little confidence in our combined abilities. If this banquet is a success, as I'm sure it will be, you'll be plagued with requests for your catering services."

She was right there, he agreed silently. With more calls for big catering jobs, he could give up the lower paying *Dinner For Two* business. But his stomach knotted at the prospect of feeding three hundred ravenous politicians.

"That's a big *if*."

"You will recall that I just raised the price from thirty-five dollars to thirty-seven fifty per plate. Let's see–two-fifty times three hundred, that's something over…"

"Seven hundred dollars," he said, finishing her sentence.

"Right. So you just leave the details to me. You concentrate on your specialty, the food."

His eyes narrowed to menacing green slits. "Leave the details to you? You, who are leaving in two weeks? You, who just accepted a house from razzy Raymond? You who will be over your head starting your own business?"

Misty pressed her lips firmly together, did an about face and marched to the front window. She extracted the HELP WANTED sign, ripped it in two, and dropped it into the trash.

(Arlene Evans)

"So much," she said, "for my replacement."

Lorna flitted around the lamp table flicking a feather duster, then placed the vase of flowers on the sparkling surface.

"Well, my goodness," she scolded her roommate, "the way you're behaving you'd think Raymond had sent you poison oak instead of these beautiful roses."

Misty observed her friend dispassionately. "I don't want anything from Raymond." That wasn't really fair to Raymond, she reasoned. The note in the card had simply said, "Let's be friends–again!"

Lorna tilted her head, regarding the flowers. "*Hmm*. Suppose Gene had given the roses to you instead?"

Misty's heart galloped with that pleasurable thought; in contrast, it had galloped that morning in pain when she saw the HELP WANTED sign in the window. But the roses! When she spied the roses, her first reaction was that Gene had placed them there for her as a romantic peace offering. He didn't want her to leave. He wanted her to stay just as much as she wanted to stay…so they could be together. She had joked about Mrs. Anderson sending the bouquet to him, but was so sure they were for her. And they were. She had been ecstatic. But when she read the card, her heart became an obstruction in her throat. They weren't from Gene. She reminded herself that gorgeous hunks were too self-centered to send flowers to women.

She smiled inwardly, thinking of how she had taken charge when the men inquired about a catered dinner.

Ordinarily more reticent, her frustration with Gene had fueled a smoldering fire resulting in an explosion of boldness. Maybe that's what's known as *chutzpah,* she thought.

With a final flick of the feather duster, Lorna noted, "Your silence says a lot. You'd be smiling if they were from Gene."

Misty gave a casual shrug of her shoulders, hoping the gesture looked convincing. "Don't be silly."

"Poor Raymond. He just wants to re-establish your old friendship. I thought the roses would do it, but apparently not."

"The roses were your idea?"

A "*Tsk*" escaped Lorna's lips. "I shouldn't talk so much, I guess." She wrung her hands and regarded her feet. "But, gee, I just wanted to help."

Misty put a hand on her friend's shoulder. "I'm just being irritable, Lorna. Actually, I'm the one who should have sent flowers to Raymond for all the trouble he went through over the Victorian. I'll call him this evening and thank him."

Lorna brightened. "Tell me something, do you think playing hard to get is the way to interest a man? I mean, well, if I played hard to get, could..." Her voice trailed off and she stared dreamily at the roses.

"I've never been one for game playing in relationships," Misty said hesitantly, "but if you weren't so...so...obvious, it might help."

Lorna pursed her lips, absorbing that information.

Gene checked an item from a list written on the legal yellow pad before him. "Okay. The menu's done, the contract is signed, and I've placed the seafood order with Artic Ocean through Sam. What next?"

Gene and Misty had finished lunch and sat making notes.

"I'll go to the annex this afternoon and sketch out the room. The staff at the Senator will set up the tables and we can order tablecloths, China, crystal and silverware from them."

Gene nodded, relieved he didn't have to be concerned about table settings.

"I discussed the banquet with the women in my class last night, and they came up with the idea of decorating and serving. A class project."

"*They* came up with the idea?" he asked skeptically.

"Close enough." Since their hike to the river with Dave and Julie's dinner, Misty had felt more self confident of her physical abilities and found that confidence spilling over into other areas of her life, like dealing with her adult students.

Gene bit the inside of his cheek. "Shouldn't we have experienced waitresses?"

"Servers," she corrected. "A few of the women have worked as servers. I'll train the rest."

Grudgingly, he admitted that at this late date, he had no choice but to accept her proposal. "That's it, then?"

"One other thing. I've set up a special file for bookkeeping purposes. Drop all receipts or other papers pertinent to the banquet in this folder."

"Yes, Your Magnificence," he teased. Damn, it had been hard working so closely with her these past weeks without touching her.

He scooted his chair closer to hers and playfully slipped an arm over the back of her chair. With his other hand, he captured her slender fingers. "It's magnificent of you to put your own business on hold until after this job is over."

She felt like shards of trembling metal being irresistibly drawn to the magnet of his body heat. With great effort, she cleared her throat, and stared straight ahead. "I expect to be magnificently paid."

He dipped his head until his mouth was close to her ear. "Of course. You'll have all the more capital to start your own business." He brushed his lips against the velvety, captivating spot below her ear.

Her heart pounding, Misty abruptly rose, knocking her chair over and throwing Gene off balance. He and his chair toppled to the floor.

Misty released a squeal of horror and dropped to her knees. Gene lay still, his strong masculine body suddenly appearing frail and vulnerable. Could he have injured his head in the fall she wondered, panic rising. Remembering her CPR training, she gently shook his shoulders and shouted, "Are you all right?"

A strong arm snaked around her waist and pulled her down on top of him. Air left her lungs in a gust of, "Oh! Let me go!"

Her protest was useless. Effectively pinned against his hard body, her heart beat wildly, every nerve at attention. She lay stiff and still as porcelain, absorbing his masculine scent. He capped the back of her head in one large hand, coaxing her lips to his. She closed her eyes as his full, sensuous lips caressed her waiting mouth. Then it was over. Grinning, he released her.

Damn his beautiful hide! He knows I wanted him to kiss me. He's toying with me. Well, I'm not a Barbie Doll to be played with.

Instead of jumping off him as he obviously expected, she combed her fingers into his hair and brought her lips down hard against his, kissing him deeply. Smiling, she rolled off him and leapt to her feet.

Gene struggled to a sitting position, then to his feet. He watched Misty hustle out the door. Well, that bit of horseplay backfired, he thought. *Damn, she's good.*

Chapter 6

Gene realized he was short on patience and long on complaints during the days immediately preceding the banquet. Worried Misty would mess up some small detail, he snapped at her like a lizard at a mosquito. And she was like a mosquito–winging around taking care of myriad chores and nipping at him, sucking his life's blood.

Yet he knew his irritation with her lay in his frustration, as if she were deliberately tantalizing him. He tried to reason with himself, saying it wasn't her fault that he felt like a teenager with raging hormones. It wasn't her fault that she was so damn attractive to him. He, and only he, was responsible for his discomfort when he fixated on the appealing mounds on her chest, or glanced at the gentle way she swished her sensuous hips. Neither was it her responsibility for the way her natural perfume traveled directly from his olfactory nerve to his gonads. Gene also lectured to himself that she wasn't flirting when she smiled in her uniquely captivating way at the male customers while anticipating their needs. She did the same for the female customers, he reasoned. Why, then, should her interaction with the males bother him so? He dismissed the notion that he could be jealous.

She knows about my multi-married family now, Gene reflected. She knows we don't do marriage well. And she knows I've remained single because I hadn't met her and I fear a long-term commitment. At least I hope she knows that, he thought. *Afraid I've inherited two bad genes–one for color vision and one for marriage!*

Misty noted Gene's edginess, which she attributed to natural tension over the upcoming banquet. She handled his uncharacteristic snaps and growls with aplomb. After all, if it weren't for her interference, he no doubt would have turned the job down. Since she was responsible for getting him into this, she could put up with his mild distemper.

In spite of his boorish behavior, however, Misty knew that Gene appreciated all the efficient, hard work she'd done. His frequent approving glances told her so better than words. Sometimes his glances unsettled her, sending waves of pleasurable discomfort coursing throughout her body. Even when he growled at her, his gruff masculine voice prickled pleasantly at her nerve endings.

Although she felt she had settled the score for his teasing kisses, the episodes still bothered her. The gentle brushes of his lips against hers left her aching for more. Why hadn't he kissed her properly she wondered. He knew she was willing. *Oh, yes, more than willing.* She sighed, thinking that she must not appeal to him in that way.

Well, why should he want her when most of the females who entered the deli fawned over him? Strange, though, that he didn't appear to flirt back. One other strange trait about Gene. He didn't behave as though he knew he were an Adonis–

"Misty, customer wants more decaf," Gene called brusquely.

Startled out of her reverie, Misty reflexed into action. Wearing her sunniest smile, she poured coffee for the lone remaining customer in the deli.

"We'll have lunch as soon as I finish this damn cake," Gene said.

The cake, laden with pastel flowers and bows, was obviously for a little girl's birthday. Misty watched as he worked, and suddenly felt like a cartoon character with a light bulb glowing above her head. Gene had described this as a "damn" cake because of all the colors. He was carefully reading labels in order to choose the correct icing color. He was colorblind! Of course. Why hadn't she realized that before? Why didn't he just simply say so and ask for help? Should she confront him with her newly discovered knowledge? She shook her head. He was obviously sensitive about the matter, so she decided to tread lightly.

"Wouldn't it be easier if I just showed you which color to use next?" she asked gently, innocently.

"I know what colors to use. I don't need any help," came the brusque response.

"Have it your way." She turned her attention to

tidying the tables.

He'd had more than enough *help* over the years, Gene thought. People who "helped" always ended up in gales of laughter and ridicule. The last time he had confided the secret of his color vision problem to someone was to a buddy in high school because he had been desperate for assistance in matching colors in the chemistry lab. His buddy helped all right, but when they had a falling out, the "friend" not only told the instructor, but everyone in the class. The news spread like a forest fire and everywhere he went people asked him colors of objects and laughed at his answers. That included those whose colorblindness wasn't as severe as his.

When the cake was boxed, Gene set out a lunch of shrimp curry and rice.

Misty leaned over her plate and inhaled deeply. "Every wonderful thing to eat reminds me of you." She nearly choked, realizing how much she sounded like all of the other wretched females who flirted with him.

"If the shrimp isn't hot enough, we can set it on your face," Gene said, a chuckle in his voice.

My cheeks must look like electric burners on high, she thought miserably. And he's probably grinning from ear to ear like the Cheshire cat. She couldn't tell for sure because her gaze was glued to her plate. She wished she could just fade away like Alice's cat.

"What was it you wanted to talk to me about?" Misty finally coughed out, still examining her food.

About how lovely you are to gaze upon, he mused, *and how your sexy voice turns me on. I'd like to talk*

126

about how fresh you smell, like a spring day after a cleansing rain.

"Well?" She was looking at him now, her cheeks having returned to their normal creamy hue.

"Uh…the banquet is less than a week away."

"Yes, I know." She raised a forkful of rice to her mouth.

"Are you ready?"

The fork halted. *Ready?* Oh, yes, she was ready. She had been for some time. Ready to run her fingers through his russet hair. Ready to make love to him. She stared at the rice and lowered her fork.

"Something wrong with the rice?"

She caught her breath. "Oh, no! I mean, no. I was just thinking about the dinner." *A lie.* "Yes, everything is going as planned. I'll be more than ready." She shoved a forkful of food in her mouth and struggled valiantly to chew.

"Anything I can help you with?"

She coughed. "No. Thanks." *Another lie. He could help her by making love to her.*

He touched her shoulder. "Are you sure you're all right?" he asked, his voice low and husky with concern. "You look pale. Are you cold?"

"Oh, I'm fine, really." She stared without appetite at her lunch. "I'm just not very hungry." *For food.* "I had a big breakfast." She scooted her chair away from the table.

"How about some hot tea?"

"Thanks, no." She stood on shaky legs and shuffled

127

behind the counter to retrieve her purse. "I really have a million details to tend to. I'll see you tomorrow."

"Sure," he responded. Recently, Gene had been taking deep breaths, a technique touted to help relieve sexual tension. It didn't seem to work, but he tried again, inhaling deeply as Misty walked out the door. If I keep this up, he thought, I'll hyperventilate.

He ate both lunches.

Misty gazed appreciatively at the group of women gathered in her apartment for a final practice session of serving. It was Thursday; the banquet was scheduled for the following Saturday. In addition to her students, Lorna and the newly engaged Julie had joined the group, insistent that they wanted to help. Misty was grateful for their eagerness and more than grateful she didn't have Mrs. Anderson to contend with. She hadn't seen the bossy, rotund woman since the abrupt ending of the *Dinner for Two* in the Anderson home. She had, however, received her past due check from Mr. Anderson for services rendered. She eagerly deposited it in her checking account to cover bills yet unpaid.

She was brought back to reality by Tulip, who interrupted her thoughts with, "Since I'm a Democrat, my boyfriend–" she giggled and blushed "–you know, the guy I sent a tulip to. Anyway, he says since this dinner is a Republican fund-raiser, I shouldn't be helping with it."

Misty's chin dropped. She couldn't afford to have anyone back out now, least of all Tulip, who had the most serving experience.

Before Misty recovered from her shock sufficiently to respond, Julie broke in: "I'm a Democrat, too, but I support our political system. There's none better."

Murmurs of approval greeted this pronouncement.

"That's a good point," Tulip admitted. "I'll tell my boyfriend that."

"Besides," Misty added, "food is non-partisan."

"That's for sure," exclaimed Henrietta, the fullest-figured woman in the group. "I'll vote for it all."

A wave of laughter rippled through the group.

Misty waited for the laughter to quiet. In recent weeks, she had been comfortable and self-assured in her role as teacher. Organizing the banquet had given her more confidence in her abilities.

She continued: "We'll meet at the annex at two Saturday afternoon. We'll put tablecloths on the tables, arrange the centerpieces, then put out the place settings. Now let's practice serving again."

Misty arranged six plates on a large round tray. "Cocktail hour starts at six. We've gone over *hors d'oeuvres* enough, I think. Precisely at seven, you'll return your trays to the kitchen and commence setting out the salads and French bread."

"Oh, it's so exciting," Henrietta said. "Just imagine, state senators and such will be there."

"How about the governor?" another asked. "Will the governor be there?"

"Ladies!" Misty tapped her foot impatiently. "You won't be there to socialize or ogle the guests. You'll be there to serve them."

"Yes, of course," Lorna agreed. "But it won't hurt, will it, if we just peek a little?"

The group tittered.

Misty ignored this latest interruption. "Give the guests plenty of time to eat," she continued. "We don't want them to feel we're rushing them. When you're sure they're finished, remove the salad plates. Quietly and discreetly. The second course is clam chowder."

"Manhattan or Boston?" Tulip asked.

"Boston."

"Good. If I spill some on anybody it won't stain."

Misty had a momentary sense of panic. Her most experienced server was considering the possibility of spilling soup on guests. Perhaps Gene had been right. Maybe they should have hired professional servers instead of these amateurs. Well, it was too late for regrets.

"After the chowder bowls are removed, you'll serve the main dishes and that's what I want you to practice now."

She hoisted the large tray with six plates on her shoulder and demonstrated balancing it with both hands. She had each one in turn lift and balance the tray then walk around the apartment. They practiced setting the tray on a stand and serving the plates. When they readied to leave, each student expressed confidence in her ability to carry and serve the meals

Misty didn't sleep well that night.

As Gene slipped the CLOSED sign in the window, he

noticed Dave walking toward the deli, little white bag in hand. He opened the door.

"Closed today?" Dave asked. "What's up?"

"The big dinner is tomorrow night. Need all day today and tomorrow to prepare. You'll have to get your own coffee."

"Oh, yeah. Julie's excited about the dinner."

"While you're at it, pour a cup for me, too. I'll need it before getting started." Gene sat in the closest chair.

Dave went to the counter, poured two cups of coffee, handed one to Gene and sat down next to him. He opened his bag and passed it to Gene.

"Have some vitamins. Keep up your energy."

Gene peered into the bag. "French doughnuts this morning?" he queried.

"A little culture never hurt anybody," Dave replied.

Gene selected one and dunked it. "So tell me how it feels to be engaged."

"It feels great. You ought to try it."

"Afraid not."

"Afraid of being tied down?"

"No, afraid the knot would slip. Knots just don't hold in my family."

"Hey, you're your own person. You tie your own knots. Don't let your family tie you down."

Their conversation was cut short by Misty's arrival. She puzzled at the sight of the two men casually dunking doughnuts.

"Excuse me," she said. "I mistook this for the deli that's catering a dinner for three hundred people tomorrow night."

Dave looked at Gene. Frowning, he said, "Is she always such a slave driver?"

Gene nodded. "It's going to be a long day, Misty. Relax for a few minutes."

She poured a cup of coffee and joined the men, declining a doughnut. They chatted briefly, then Dave arose and announced his intention of going to work.

"Have to clip my customers," he said. "Besides, you guys have unfinished business to attend to." He winked at Gene. He added, "Good luck tomorrow night."

Dave's wink was lost on Misty, but she squirmed uncomfortably, suspecting it had something to do with her.

Gene and Misty lingered only a moment more at the table before retreating to behind the counter to commence work. Misty gathered purple cabbage and green onions and started mincing. She'd be able to assist him all day, and the next morning as well. Then she'd take some of the food to the annex to refrigerate it before meeting with her crew.

Gene figured he'd be up at least until midnight preparing the seafood Sam had delivered that morning. He hoped to catch a few Zs before starting work again early Saturday morning. Beside him, Misty worked quietly, efficiently. Normally chatty, she seemed to sense his need for silence. Not that stillness equated to tranquility, but it helped. And he needed all the tranquility he could muster. Maybe she needed it, too.

In spite of the dominant odor of shellfish surrounding

them, he could detect her fresh, clear scent. Did she wear perfume, he wondered, or was hers just a clean, soapy smell? Her skin was polished to a glowing hue and her hair was like a black sky twinkling with stars. Oh, hell, he had to stop thinking about her and how horny he was and concentrate on the food preparation.

Frequently, Misty found herself glancing at the man next to her with an inexplicable longing. Emulating Gene's skill with the chef's knife, she imagined his hands on her waist. She shuddered. Her arms roughened with goose bumps.

"Cold?" Gene asked.

She stifled a laugh, wondering what he'd do if she told him why she had just shuddered. Would he immediately cease his activities and wrap his arms around her? No, she reasoned, he's too sensible for that. He'd just continue mincing and tell her he'd take a rain check.

"Want me to turn on the heat?" Gene asked.

"No, no, I'm fine, really. I'm not cold at all."

Too bad. I'd be only too happy to warm you up.

They had worked for several hours when the door burst open and Lorna breezed through.

I knew I should have locked that door, Gene thought. The CLOSED sign wasn't enough to keep her out.

"You need any help?"

Misty glanced at her fair-complexioned roommate whose newly spiral-permed hair rested squarely on her shoulders.

"Your hair looks great!"

"Thanks." She whirled around. "Does it look okay

in the back?"

Gene grunted.

"It's beautiful in the back," Misty responded.

Nonplused, Gene shook his head. Women with straight hair were always frizzing it up and women with curly hair were ironing theirs flat. It didn't make any sense.

Misty turned to Gene. "I think we have everything under control, don't we?"

Gene gave an abrupt nod of his head. "Sure. And I can't stop to fix lunch."

Misty narrowed her dark eyes at his rude remark and glared at his ruddy face.

Lorna stepped closer to the counter to observe the work in progress. "I've already had lunch. At a restaurant near the beauty parlor. Just thought I'd stop by to see how you two were doing."

"That was nice of you. Gene, don't you think that was nice of Lorna?"

Okay, be civil, Gene instructed himself. Just because you're half-crazy with lust doesn't mean you can't be pleasant.

He stopped chopping and actually looked at Lorna. She *was* kind of cute with her hair curled, he conceded. All in all, a nice-looking girl. But it was dark-haired Misty who caused the tightness in his chest and other parts.

"Your hair looks great, Lorna. And thanks for coming by." To make his thanks sound more genuine, he asked, "Can we call you if we need your help?"

"Please do." She turned to Misty. "You don't mind if I serve Raymond's table tomorrow night, do you Misty? I mean, the other women don't mind."

"Raymond's going to be there?" Gene asked.

"Oh, yes. He's very active in the Young Republicans."

Gene wondered if Raymond's presence was the reason for Lorna's new hairdo. At least, being in the kitchen, he wouldn't have to put up with seeing the creep.

"I don't mind," Misty said, "as long as you don't give Raymond any more attention than you do the other guests."

"Trust me, I won't. Toodle-do." She breezed out.

"'Toodle-do?'" Gene repeated.

With firm pursed lips, Misty said, "You needn't be sarcastic. She did volunteer to help us, you know."

"Right. But would she have if Raymond weren't going to be there?"

Annoyed with his innuendo, Misty brought her knife down hard, slicing though the nail on her left index finger.

"Ouch! Darn it!"

Gene dropped his knife. In two quick steps he was at Misty's side, taking possession of her hand. A drop of blood oozed out from under the sliced nail. With an arm around her shoulders he scooted her to the sink, turned on the cold water, and moved her hand until the injured finger was directly under the running stream.

"Keep it there," he directed. He vanished, then reappeared with an anti-bacterial ointment and Band-

Aids. He washed the wound, dried it, and applied the dressing.

Although perfectly capable of taking care of her own wound, Misty submitted meekly to Gene's ministrations. And yes, she admitted, she enjoyed the whole process. He treated her hand as delicately as he folded a soufflé.

When he finished applying the Band-Aid, Gene was reluctant to release her hand. He glanced at her face, then looked into eyes that gazed intently into his.

Misty's breathing grew deeper, more rapid. She wanted him to take her other hand, to draw her close to him. She wanted to nuzzle and kiss his freckle-splashed neck. She wanted to feel his hands crushing her body to his.

Gene sighed and wet his lips. He lifted her bandaged finger to his mouth. He ached to taste all those fingers, but instead planed a quick kiss on the injured finger. "There. Now it'll be all better."

Exasperated, Misty pulled her hand away. Imagine kissing her injured finger like he would a child's! Silently grousing, she thought that must be the way he thinks of her–as a child. She slipped a plastic glove over her hand and returned to her vegetables, mincing with a vengeance.

Chapter 7

The Senator Annex was well lit by shimmering chandeliers that sparkled in the several strategically located decorative mirrors. Off-white, textured paper clothed the walls, and an earth-toned carpet covered the floors. The round tables were perfectly arranged, topped by white tablecloths, with red, white, and blue streamers strewn artistically across them. Centerpieces were silver-colored balls with several American flag through each.

Misty looked approvingly at the room, then at her crew of servers. As directed, they wore black trousers and long-sleeved white blouses. Those with long hair had it pulled back into buns or French braids. Lorna's newly permed hair was swooped to the sides and fastened with combs.

The women murmured anxiously among themselves, eager for the guests to arrive.

Misty went into the kitchen where Gene was putting the finishing touches on trays of appetizers. She walked past the trays, lined up on a sideboard. "They look wonderful," she said. *So do you.* "You do use colors in unique ways."

Gene glanced up sharply. "What do you mean?" he asked, a defensive tone in his voice. "Aren't the colors natural looking?"

"Not natural, necessarily, but certainly very festive…and attractive."

Pacified, he said, "Oh."

Henrietta and Tulip poked their heads into the kitchen.

"They're arriving," Tulip exclaimed, a wide smile on her face. "And guess what–the governor just drove up!"

Gene's heart thumped, then dropped down to his stomach. This dinner had to go well. If it didn't, he'd be ruined. He might as well close the deli.

"Both of you take a tray of appetizers," Misty directed, "and start circulating."

Within the next few minutes, each of the other servers came to the kitchen to secure a tray of appetizers. Misty left the kitchen momentarily to observe her crew at work. She was heartened to see Lorna serving guests in one corner of the room while Raymond was with a group of people in the opposite corner. Her fears about Lorna concentrating on Raymond were unfounded, she concluded.

Glancing to the front entrance, she suddenly stiffened with horror. The Andersons arrived! The gaunt Jason Anderson helped his corpulent wife remove her billowy gray cape. *Jack Sprat and his wife.*

Quickly, before they spotted her, Misty escaped to the kitchen.

"What's wrong?" Gene demanded, looking at her stark-white face.

She hesitated telling him, but felt he had a right to know. "The Andersons are here," she said, one hand pressed against her chest.

Gene guffawed. "They obviously didn't know who was preparing this dinner. That's their problem. Don't give them a second thought."

Not giving them a second thought was difficult to do. Misty relaxed somewhat, but couldn't help feeling that the Andersons' presence was a bad omen.

Attempting to distract her, Gene asked, "How are our girls doing?"

"The *servers* are doing marvelously. How are you doing?"

He gave the chowder a hearty stir with a long-handled wooden spoon. "Everything seems to be under control," he said, hardly believing his statement himself.

"Inside as well as out?"

Her concern for his emotional state warmed him like Boston chowder. "Yeah, I'm okay. How about you?"

"Now that we've actually started, the butterflies have settled."

They reflected each other's smiles, their gazes lingering. Gene broke the spell by returning his attention to the stove.

At precisely seven, the servers returned their trays to the kitchen and began setting out salads and French bread. By seven-thirty the clam chowder was ladled into warmed bowls, ready for serving. Holding her breath, Misty watched with wide eyes as the servers hoisted their trays of chowder and carried them out to the dining room. Please don't let them spill any on the diners, she prayed silently. She stepped into the dining room quickly to oversee the operation and heard no shrieks of pain or horror, so assumed her prayer was answered.

"Everyone loves the chowder," Henrietta announced as she passed by Misty.

Misty returned to the kitchen and related Henrietta's message. "So far, everything's going like clockwork," she added.

Together, Gene and Misty filled bowls of cracked crab for the servers to set on the tables for the celebrants to help themselves. Then they arranged Gene's specialty dishes on dinner plates, which the servers efficiently whisked away.

While the guests continued eating, the master of ceremonies took over the microphone. Busy in the kitchen readying the dessert, Gene and Misty could hear only a muffled voice. But then the sound of stomping feet and cries of "Chef! Chef!" came across loud and clear.

"They want to see you," Misty said, excitement trilling her voice. "Go out!"

Gene hesitated. "Come with me. I couldn't have done it without you."

"No. You're the chef." She straightened his chef's hat and gave him a firm push. "Now go!"

When Gene emerged from the kitchen's swinging doors into the dining room, cheers and applause greeted him. He swooped off his hat and bowed deeply.

When he straightened, two men with surly eyes who were not joining in the applause came into his view. Jason Anderson and Raymond. They *would* be seated at the same table, he thought. Probably exchanging war stories about me and hoping I'll fall flat on my face. The clapping continued, so he waved, then returned to the kitchen.

"Your career is launched," Misty exclaimed.

He grasped both her shoulders. "Thanks to you." He pulled her to him and kissed her firmly on the lips. Then he released her, patted her invitingly rounded derriere, and turned his attention to the dessert.

Lordy, he's done it again. Launches me into orbit with a kiss and leaves me circling the globe. Trembling, Misty picked up a spatula to help dish up strawberry pie.

Gene moved past her, brushing his thigh against the back of hers. *Why can't I keep from touching her?*

The arrival of Lorna and Julie with trays of dirty dishes derailed Gene's train of thought. Then the other servers arrived, similarly burdened. After setting down their trays, the women squirted dollops of whipped cream on the slices of pie, then served them.

Amid droning speeches by the various politicians, a special clean-up crew that was included in the rental of the annex arrived and began washing dishes.

"Guess we'd better feed the waitresses," Gene said. "You hungry?"

"No. I'm strung taut. I couldn't eat a thing."

Other than tasting food to correct seasonings, he'd been too busy to eat all day and found himself without an appetite now.

He lined up plates of food for the crew. When the servers returned to the kitchen, they found their dinners waiting and dug into the bountiful fare.

"Great work, ladies," Gene commended. He picked up a pot of coffee in each hand. "You gals stay here and enjoy your meal. I'll go around with coffee refills."

"I'll help," Misty said. She hugged each woman in turn, then rushed out to help Gene.

Misty and Gene were greeted with copious messages of praise and remarks like, "Where's your restaurant?" and "Do you have a business card?"

Misty went to the table where Raymond sat and saw no sign of the Andersons.

"Did the Andersons leave?" she asked Raymond.

"Yes. Shortly after the chef made his appearance. Jason said he'd lost his appetite, but he doesn't look like he's ever had one." He chuckled. "His wife was upset about leaving before dessert."

An ominous feeling returned to Misty, causing her skin to prickle unpleasantly. You're imagining things, she scolded herself.

When the diners were sated, the speeches finally done, and the clean up complete, the happy servers bade farewell while the chef and *sous chef* loaded equipment in their respective vehicles.

"Meet you at the deli," Misty called as she pulled away from the curb. What a day! What an evening! She couldn't have asked for a more successful dinner, yet an annoying gloom shadowed her happiness.

On a high from the successful dinner, Gene waved to Misty and sailed, rather than drove, to the deli.

With identical wide grins that mirrored their moods, the pair unloaded the equipment.

Misty breathed a sigh of relief when she set the last load on the counter. "I can't believe it's really over."

His back to Misty, Gene murmured in an uncharacteristically soft voice, "We did it." He turned to face her squarely then raised his voice in pitch and volume to bellow, "By damn, we actually did it!" He closed the distance between them, fastened his hands around her waist, and raised her high over his head as if she were an umbrella.

"*Oh*," Misty squeaked with delight. Hands on his shoulders, arms straight, she looked down into his lush, verdant eyes.

Joyously, Gene swung her around in a wide circle like a merry-go-round gone wild. Suddenly, noting a change in her expression from joyous to lustful, he stopped in mid swing. The happy grin had left her lovely face; her sparkling eyes, so full of exuberance just a moment before, had softened to dark, sensual pools. Careful, he cautioned himself. His own mood had changed from playfulness to acute awareness of her nearness, of his hands circling her alluring body.

Luxuriating in her sensual gaze, he lowered her, sliding her down the length of his body. His lungs turned to gelatin as her breasts brushed against his chest. When her feet touched the floor, she made no move to take her hands from his shoulders. Save for their breathing, silence reined.

Standing statue still, their gazes entwined, his hands rested on her hips. He wanted to kiss her, caress her, to make love to her as he had so often dreamed of doing. He knew she was ripe for his kisses, she was his for the plucking, but he also knew he had nothing to offer her except an affair.

He resolved to put her from him, but her hands slid to the back of his neck, then tightened. His head slowly lowered. She raised herself on her toes to touch her lips to his. Oh, lord, he groaned inwardly, just one kiss. *One kiss and I'll let her go.*

Winding his arms tightly around her, he bent his head to take firm possession of her eager mouth. He drank in her sweetness as he would dessert, then broke the kiss, resolving not to meet her lips again. Ah, he'd just nibble at her chin that jutted up coquettishly toward him, he thought. But she tilted her head, offering him full access to her soft, tapered neck. He worked his way down the creamy length of her neck with long, slow kisses. She made appreciative sounds from deep within in her throat.

"Misty," he breathed, wanting her to stop him, and praying she wouldn't. He willed her to leave him before it was too late. He willed her to stay.

She placed her hands on either side of his face, directing his lips back to hers. He knew he was like the Titanic, sinking fast.

Like a drowning man desperate for air, he was suddenly delirious with the need to have contact with her bare skin. He tugged her blouse out from the waistband of her trousers, and slid his hands underneath. Soft and smooth as satin, just as he knew her skin would be.

Slipping his hands up her back, he unfastened her bra and brought a hand around to cover one breast. She gasped and bit gently on his lower lip, her hands kneading his back.

He wanted her hands on his bare skin, too. "I don't have fancy digs to offer you," he murmured.

In answer, she smiled, took his hand, and led him into his bedroom. He switched on his bedside lamp and watched with patience and pleasure while she unbuttoned her blouse, then shrugged it off along with her bra. She sat on his bed and he quickly knelt beside her to remove her shoes and socks. He leaned over her lap to grasp her around the waist, then kissed her abdomen.

She gasped. "Gene, please...let me undress."

"Gladly." He unfastened her pants and she wiggled out of them. Then he slid her panties off. Perfect. She was perfectly beautiful, like a live porcelain doll.

Impatient with his own clothing, Gene tore off his things and dropped them in a heap by the side of the bed. He wanted to ask her if she was on the pill, but it seemed like too personal a question. Instead, he fished a condom out of his bedside stand, hoping it wasn't outdated. Then he was lying next to her, caressing every part of her body, and enjoying the touch of her delicate hands on his hot skin.

His need was great, but he cautioned himself to take it easy, to be sure that she was ready. She wasn't helping on that score, though, with her body writhing seductively and mewing sounds emanating from deep within her throat. Then her hands slipped down to caress his hardened shaft. Well, he wondered, just how much is a man supposed to endure. He rolled on the prophylactic, grateful it was still moist and resilient, then adjusted his body between her parting thighs. Losing all control, he entered her with a single, powerful thrust.

"*Oh,*" she cried, tensing.

Shocked, he asked, "Did I hurt you?"

Her body softened. "No, I was just startled. You feel wonderful." She caressed his neck and shoulders, her hips beginning a slow rotation in rhythm to his thrusts.

Gene wanted to prolong the lovemaking, but again, Misty wasn't helping. Her hands grazed over his tingling skin and her pelvic movements titillated him further. Finally, intoxicated beyond control, he reached climax, then stayed firmly against her until her body, too, achieved its release. Exhausted, he relaxed on top of her. Dozing, he awakened slowly and realized he must be crushing her.

He slid off her. Her body felt as limp as a Raggedy Anne.

They lay still and silent for several minutes, then Misty kissed Gene's neck and began toying with his wiry chest hair. She released a low chuckle.

"What's so funny?"

She hesitated before confessing. "The first time I saw you I wondered if all your body hair was the same color."

"So that's the reason you seduced me."

146

"Exactly."

"And did you get a good look?"

"I made sure of it."

"And a good enough feel?"

"*Mm hmm*. I found out that this hair," she pulled a tuft of his chest hair, "feels just like this hair." She moved her hand to his pubic area.

He exhaled a moan and was surprised to feel himself harden again so soon. Given the chance, he reasoned, starving men will overeat.

They made love again, then scooted under the covers, and fell asleep.

Misty awoke slowly, luxuriating in the memory of a perfect night of lovemaking. She blinked her eyes open to see Gene, propped on one elbow, looking down at her, a serious expression on his face.

Her joy quickly vanished. Dread obstructed her throat. He's sorry we made love, she concluded, but she managed a perky, "Good morning."

"It was a great night," he said.

His words sounded right, but his inflection was wrong. "Yes, the banquet was a bigger success than either of us could have imagined."

"That's not what I meant and you know it." He rolled over to his back, a bent arm resting on his forehead.

"Well, perhaps you should stop the delaying tactics and simply tell me what's on your mind."

"Marriage."

She held her breath. Was he going to propose? She realized, without surprise, that she would welcome a proposal. She loved this man, and had loved him for a very long time. She imagined waking up each morning, Gene at her side. She thought pleasantly of making a home with him. She pictured working side by side with him, building, and improving *their* business. Then she imagined being the mother of his children and felt warm to the core of her being.

"Marriages don't work in my family, at least not for long," he continued.

Her enchanting mental pictures disappeared as if covered by one whoosh of a roller brush. "I see," she murmured.

"No, you don't. Your family was always stable. You don't know what it's like living in a home where step-fathers come and go through a revolving door."

Momentarily shocked into silence, Misty sat up, rotating her body until her feet touched the floor. "Because we spent the night together, you assume that I expect you to do the honorable thing and marry me?" she asked in a voice heavy with sarcasm. "Isn't that rather old-fashioned and presumptuous?"

"You're not the kind of girl–"

"You obviously don't know what kind of *woman* I am. I'm certainly not the kind to have revolving door step-fathers for my children." Feeling very naked, she snatched her clothing, held the bundle in front of her, and sprinted to the bathroom. When she emerged fully dressed, Gene was sitting on the side of the bed, the covers tossed aside.

What kind of a woman am I? How could a man who

was so insulting to me just moments before look so delicious? She wanted to strip and re-join him on the bed.

Gene glanced up at her. "I didn't mean you'd be that way, Misty. I didn't mean you'd be irresponsible. It's me I'm worried about. Just look at my family history," he said. "My sister and brother are as bad as my mother. Why–"

"Oh, please spare me any more of your dribble!" Furious, she swallowed hard, knowing that the next part of her little speech would be a lie. "I have no desire to be married at this point in my life, so you needn't try to salve your conscience about tainting my honor."

Gene stood, his magnificent bulk overwhelming all her senses. He extended a hand to her. "We can still be friends?"

"Why not?"

Ignoring his outstretched hand, she did an about-face and marched out the door.

Chapter 8

Acutely aware of her anger and pain, Misty drove home with more than her usual caution. She pulled into her parking spot at the apartment complex determined not to shed any of the tears that filmed her vision. She cut the engine

How could she have fallen in love with such a man? Another gorgeous man who considered only himself? He actually expected her to believe his family had what–a divorce gene? How absurd. How ridiculous. How humiliating!

She shook her head violently, as if to shake out any thoughts of him. Why couldn't he just be honest and say he didn't want to be stuck with her? Yet, she admitted she had no one to blame but herself for falling in love with the man. Nor could she blame him for what had happened the night before. He hadn't tried to seduce her. Oh, no, she had been a most active, assertive participant.

With a balled fist, she pounded her frustration into the steering wheel. Then, totally spent she felt like a music box that had wound down. With a deep sigh, she lowered the visor and took a quick peek at herself in the mirror. She didn't want to face Lorna looking like she'd been attacked by a hurricane, although that was exactly the way she felt. She smoothed her hair with her hands. There was nothing she could do about the sunburned look of her face, the result of Gene's sand paper whiskers.

Misty glanced at her watch–good–only seven. Lorna would still be sleeping. She'd be able to sneak into her bedroom without her roommate being any the wiser. She struggled out of her car and up the front steps.

Misty was shocked to find the apartment door unlocked. She'd have to speak to Lorna about being more careful about securing the apartment before going to bed. Another shock awaited her–Lorna, dressed in her server outfit of black pants and white blouse, was in the kitchen making coffee.

Spying her roommate, Lorna startled, spilling coffee grounds on the kitchen counter. "Well, my goodness, I thought you were in bed. Wherever have you been?"

"I might ask you the same question," Misty replied. "You just got home yourself, didn't you?"

"Well, er...sort of."

"You were with Raymond?" Misty asked.

"And you were with Gene." Lorna paused, scrutinizing her friend's sad, abraded face. "The night didn't go well?"

Misty collapsed in a kitchen chair. Remembering the pleasurable night, an unbidden smile upturned the corners of her lips. "The night was wonderful. But this morning left a great deal to be desired." Her lips assumed a down-turned position. "How was your night?"

Lorna's cheeks pinked. "It was lovely. And he's going to pick me up this afternoon. We're going to his club to play tennis."

A twinge of envy jabbed at Misty. Raymond and Lorna still had a relationship after spending a night together.

Lorna placed a cup of steaming coffee in front of her friend. "Tell me about your morning," she said.

Misty sighed. "He wanted to be very sure I understood he didn't have marriage in mind. Presumptuous, chauvinistic male!"

Uncharacteristically silent, Lorna looked askance at her friend while stirring skim milk and a teaspoon of sugar into her coffee.

"He thinks I was trying to trap him into marriage."

"Maybe he has an old fashioned conscience," Lorna offered. "You know, when you go to bed with a girl you're supposed to marry her."

"That's an insulting attitude, as if I had been naive enough to be tricked into making love." On the other hand, maybe he feels he was tricked into making love, Misty considered. She tried unsuccessfully to dismiss that thought.

Lorna squeezed Misty's arm. "He'll realize what he said is foolish, just see if he doesn't. Then he'll be on the phone to you."

Misty shook her head. "No, I don't think so. He was raving on about his family and how none of them have ever had successful marriages."

"Well, my goodness, no wonder he's so upset about falling in love," Lorna exclaimed. "He's concerned that both he and his beloved–that's you–will be hurt." She crossed her hands over her heart. "That's *sooo* romantic."

Misty rolled her eyes, thinking her roommate should have had a career on the stage. Yet she wanted to believe in Lorna's histrionics. Was it possible that Gene had fallen in love with her? She shook her head. No, not hardly.

"I'm afraid his family trait is just an excuse he used to let me know his only abiding interest in me is as an employee. And an occasional bedmate."

"That's just not so. Don't be so hard on him. Like I've said before, he's crazy about you. I can see it."

Misty couldn't bear talking about Gene any longer. "How do you feel about Raymond?" she asked.

Dreamy-eyed, Lorna stirred her coffee then took a sip. "My feelings about him have certainly changed."

"Yes, I recall the time you were suspicious of a weird glint in his eye."

Lorna giggled. "That glint is really quite romantic."

"But do you love him?"

"It's a little too soon to say," she hedged, "but I certainly do...well, like him an awful lot."

Misty smiled. "I'm happy for you. I hope it all works out the way you want it to."

The phone rang.

"I'll just bet that's Gene now," Lorna said.

Misty tensed. *Could it be...?*

Lorna answered. "Oh, hi, Raymond." She looked at

Misty, raising her eyebrows apologetically, then turned her attention to the telephone. Smiling broadly, she twirled one of her spiral curls with an index finger.

Misty sighed.

Lorna's smile gradually faded, replaced by thin lips, and puckered brows. She mumbled some words Misty couldn't catch. When she cradled the receiver, she stood statue still, staring straight ahead.

If Raymond has hurt Lorna, I'll commit mayhem, Misty pledged. She went to her friend, put an arm around her shoulders, and led her to the couch.

"Tell me about it," Misty urged.

Eyes downcast, Lorna said, "If he doesn't want to see me again, I wish he'd just say so."

Misty harrumphed. That sentiment sounded familiar. "What did he say?"

"He says he doesn't feel well. He has a stomachache. He thinks Gene poisoned him last night."

Such drama was so typical of Raymond, Misty thought, disgusted. "He's always had a delicate stomach," she said. "As a kid he was forever complaining about stomachaches." Especially when he wanted to get out of something, she thought wryly.

So, she and Lorna had both spent the night with heels. She hoped, if nothing else, that their experiences would be learning tools they could call on for future use.

She caught her breath, wondering how she was to face Gene the next day. She considered not going in to work at all, but she didn't want him to know how deeply she was affected by his rebuff. Also, she scolded herself, she shouldn't let her emotions interfere with her obligations to her employer. Under the circumstances, though, she obviously couldn't go on working with him. She'd give her two weeks' notice and make it stick this time.

"You know something," Lorna said, "I don't feel so hot, either. My tummy is kind of...well, sickish."

An emotional reaction to Raymond's rebuff, Misty concluded. "We have some of that soothing pink stuff. Why don't you take a dose and lie down?"

"Yes, I think I will."

Jogging along the levee early Monday morning, Gene took deep, full breaths to clear his lungs and undo the tangled thoughts knotting up his head. The lungs were doing okay, but his brain remained addled.

He'd spent the day before cleaning up from the banquet and getting the deli in shape for another week. Usually when he was emotionally disturbed, he'd stuff his gullet. But, for the first time in memory, food held no appeal. His belly not only rejected the idea of nourishment, it found food odors nauseating.

He determined that his physical discomforts were the result of Misty's anger. She didn't believe him. She dismissed his multiply married family as if they didn't exist. She though he just wanted to be rid of her. Well, he could hardly believe his family, either. None of them had known lasting love or caring.

Would she show up for work today, he wondered. He wouldn't blame her if she didn't. On one hand, he knew it was best if she didn't show—he had nothing to offer her in the way of a permanent relationship, and that's what she deserved. On the other hand, he couldn't imagine not seeing her again.

His abdomen grumbled. The discomfort he had experienced in his belly the day before seemed to be descending into his intestines. If she's the cause of all this inner growling and grumbling, he tried to convince himself, I'm better off without her.

When he arrived back at the deli, Gene showered, shaved, and started to dress when the phone rang. His chest constricted. It was too early for a customer to call. He assumed the caller was Misty, about to tell him she wouldn't be in. He lifted the receiver, dreading the thought of hearing her low, sexy voice.

"*Dinner for Two*," he answered.

"Gene Haynes?" the male voice queried.

Gene exhaled slowly, his chest loosening. "Yes."

"You did the banquet at the Republican fund raiser Saturday evening?"

Ah, all that hard work is paying off, Gene thought. This guy was referred to me because of the resounding success of the banquet. He probably wants to schedule another one. Maybe I can persuade Misty to help.

"Sure did."

The caller cleared his throat. "This is Mike de Maio, sanitarian with the County Health Department."

Gene's euphoria abruptly disappeared, replaced by apprehension. "Time for an inspection?" He hoped that was the case.

"Afraid it's a little more than that."

Gene's apprehension deepened. "Go on."

"We've had reports from a few physicians," de Maio continued, "regarding several patients that were treated yesterday. The patients had symptoms of possible food poisoning, and they all had one thing in common: they ate your dinner Saturday night."

Gene held his breath, his intestines rattling.

"Are you still there, Mr. Haynes?"

"Yes, I'm still here." Unfortunately, he thought. Food poisoning. A chef's worst nightmare. He wanted the floor to swallow him whole. "The people affected–are they okay? Anybody hospitalized?"

"That part's the good news. The symptoms are mild. Some nausea and diarrhea. In some of the cases, the doctors didn't even see the patients, just reassured them."

"Glad to hear that at least. How can I help?"

"I need to come over and see your place today and ask you a few questions. Do you have any leftovers from the dinner?"

"No. Sorry. We had a lot of food, but the diners ate almost everything. We dumped the rest."

"That's okay. We'll try to identify the organism by examining patients' stool samples."

Now there's a job I wouldn't want, Gene thought, although it might be better than being a chef.

"I'll be over in a couple of hours," the sanitarian concluded.

Gene cradled the receiver. Mentally, he went over all his food preparation activities. He couldn't think of a single instance where he could possibly have contaminated anything. Everything that needed to be kept cold was on ice from start to finish. Maybe it was all a big mistake. Or, just a coincidence that several people became ill. The sanitarian did say several. There were three hundred guests at the banquet, after all. "Several" isn't a big percentage of three hundred. Maybe it wasn't food poisoning. Maybe the "several" just overate. Or drank too much.

His intestines audibly complained. Is food poisoning my problem, he worried. Misty isn't the cause of my growling gut after all? Misty! Is she all right? Suppose she's sick? He had to find out. He grabbed the receiver and punched in her number.

Her sultry voice answered, "Hullo," reminding Gene of the first time he had spoken with her.

"Misty, it's Gene. Are you okay?"

His voice sounded hurried and anxious. But what does he mean, am I okay? He must think I'm pining away because of his rejection. Emotionally destitute. Well, I'll show him.

"Of course I'm okay. Why wouldn't I be?" she snapped.

She may be all right physically, but she's still mad as hell at me, Gene thought wryly. He related the substance of the call from the health department sanitarian, and he wondered if she was ill at all.

"Oh," Misty breathed, "so that's what's wrong with Lorna."

"Lorna's sick?"

"Yes. When she first complained of a stomachache yesterday I thought it was due to an emotional upset. But she wasn't feeling any better in the evening and this morning she's…uh, going to the bathroom a lot."

Aargh, Gene thought. Just like me, only mine's milder. "You didn't eat much Saturday, did you?"

"No. I was too jumpy." She had managed to eat a piece of pie, however. "You didn't eat, either."

"But I did taste everything prior to the banquet to correct the seasonings."

"And you're not sick?"

"A little queasy is all."

"Everything in the deli is so sanitary," Misty protested. "Your technique is impeccable." How could she be praising him, she wondered, after his detestable behavior. "And all the food was refrigerated until the last minute. How could this have happened?"

"That's what I'm asking myself."

They were both silent for a long moment. "So how do the officials handle a situation like this?" she asked at last.

"A sanitarian is coming over to inspect the place and I assume to ask a bunch of questions."

"I'll be over, too," Misty said. "After I call the servers. I want to be sure they're all okay."

Misty arrived at the deli on the heels of the sanitarian. Pushing seven feet, the broad-shouldered man was casually dressed in slacks and an aloha shirt. He carried an official-looking briefcase.

After introductions, de Maio began a meticulous

inquiry into the manner of food preparation for the banquet as well as food storage before serving. Thoughtfully, Gene answered the questions, endeavoring to recall every detail.

"You're sure you don't have any leftovers?" he asked.

"None," Gene said.

Misty asked, "Don't people get sick immediately from food poisoning?"

"Food poisoning can be caused by a number of organisms, each with different incubation periods." He turned to Gene. "Where did you purchase the seafood?"

"From the Arctic Ocean Seafood Suppliers in Seattle. I've bought seafood from them before and haven't had a problem."

Nodding, the sanitarian jotted notes on a yellow pad. "*Hmm*. Seattle. I'll have to notify the State Department of Heath."

"You're not going to close the deli, are you?" Misty asked apprehensively.

Gene warmed with her concern.

"No, not at all. You can carry on as usual for now."

Muttering under his breath, Gene said, "But who the hell will come here to eat once the word gets around?"

"Thank you both for your cooperation," de Maio said at last. "If you hear of any new cases, be sure to have them call the health department. We'll need to get a history on every affected person." He fished a business card out of his wallet and handed it to Gene.

"We'll do that," Gene said.

The sanitarian picked up his briefcase and left.

Misty looked so distressed that Gene wanted to enfold her in his arms to comfort her. Yet, she seemed constrained, untouchable. He said, "Thanks for coming. I appreciate the support."

She knew he must be emotionally tormented by this turn of events and she wanted to console him, even if he was a louse. "I hope I helped."

Gene thought he'd need a cleaver to hack away the tension between them. He had never known her to be cool and reserved the way she seemed now. Her real nature was warm and giving.

"How are the servers?" he asked.

"Tulip and Henrietta are a little ill, but everybody else is fine. Actually, Henrietta is tickled. She hopes she'll lose a couple of pounds."

"Tough way to diet. Better have them call the health department."

"Yes, I will." Misty averted her gaze from his. The food poisoning issue had temporarily distracted her from her anger and pain, but now she felt their full emotional impact once again. She steeled herself for what she was about to say.

"Under the circumstances," she began slowly, "I feel it best to tender my resignation."

His stomach clenched, and he knew it wasn't due to food poisoning. "I was afraid of that. I'll miss you. And your decorations."

I'll miss you, too. As angry as she was, she knew she still loved this man. Deeply and fully. "As I've said before, I believe a man and a woman need to maintain a professional relationship if they're to work together successfully."

He nodded, as if in agreement, but wondered if that was always the case. "You'll be opening your own business in the Victorian?"

"No, I chose not to be in Raymond's debt. Perhaps I'll find a position with a florist until I can afford a business loan."

At least she won't be around that scumbag Raymond, he thought. "You're welcome to stay here as long as it takes to find the right job."

"Thanks, but I think two weeks will be ample time."

She can hardly wait to get out. "If you find something before the two weeks are up, I won't hold you."

He can hardly wait to be rid of me. She decided to start job-hunting that afternoon.

In spite of a brisk lunch business, the day dragged for Gene. Overtly, he watched Misty, and was alarmed by an agonizing torment in his chest.

When the last customer left, he said, "I'll have lunch for us in a jiffy."

"No, thank you. I need to be on my way," she said, hating to leave and not wanting to look for another job.

He wondered if the disappointment he felt showed on his face. He had always looked forward to their lunches together. It was the high point of his day. He'd miss their bantering. He'd miss the sight, sound, and scent of her. He'd miss her.

Misty tucked her purse under her arm and headed for the door. She opened the door and halted in mid stride.

"There's a TV crew headed this way!"

"Huh?"

She waved one arm. "Look at that van."

Gene joined her at the door. Sure enough, a van emblazoned with the logo of a local TV station was parked across the street. A guy with a video camera hoisted on his shoulder and a woman with a reporter's notebook jaywalked, heading directly for his place.

Groaning, Gene said, "I guess it's too much to hope that we'll be getting some free publicity for the great dinner we cooked and served Saturday night."

"That would be good news," Misty responded. "Who wants to see good news on TV?"

The TV duo halted outside the deli while the photographer shot some footage. Gene quickly closed the door so he and Misty wouldn't be caught on film. To no avail. The news team then entered the deli, camera rolling.

"Hi," the woman with the notebook said. "I'm Jan Woods and the photographer is Dennis Bradley. We'd like to ask you a few questions about your dinner Saturday night."

Wary, Gene asked, "Why?"

"We had a report about food poisoning."

"Surely a few cases of food poisoning aren't feature news material." Gene hoped not, anyway.

"A few?" the reporter repeated. "How about thirty-four and rising?"

"Thirty-four?" Gene said, stunned.

"And since both the governor and the mayor are

affected, believe me, it's news."

"Both the governor and the mayor are sick?" Misty asked, incredulous.

"You hadn't heard?"

Gene shook his head. "A health department official was here this morning, but obviously statistics have changed since then."

"Obviously," the reporter repeated. "We'd like to know what, exactly, you served."

Just then, the door swung open and another couple, clones of the already present TV pair, entered.

"Thought you'd scoop us, didn't you?" the new arrival said, opening her notebook.

"Fat chance," the first reporter said.

The two women began firing questions at Gene.

As much as he would have liked to throw the foursome out, Gene saw no point in being uncooperative. Reluctantly, he answered the reporters' questions.

Misty, standing well out of the camera's range, felt bewildered by the recent events. Her anger at Gene had dissipated, replaced by empathy for the ordeal he was experiencing. Yet he was handling the situation with all the masculine dignity inherent in him.

Gene sighed with relief when at last he held the door open for the TV crews to exit. Then he spied a young man in a photo vest wearing a jaunty fishing hat with a press card upended in the band walking briskly toward the deli.

"Hell, no," Gene said. "No more today!" He slammed the door, locked it, turned his cardboard sign over from OPEN to CLOSED, then shut the blinds.

Chapter 9

Misty and Lorna sat in their living room, their attention riveted to the five o'clock TV news.

"The Grand Old Party had a Gastronomically Over-Priced seafood dinner Saturday night," the commentator began.

"Oh, no," Misty moaned. "They're going to make a joke out of it. It was no joke!"

"…and we understand the Democrats are saying the Republicans got their just desserts."

"Ha," Lorna huffed. "You can tell he wasn't the one trotting to the bathroom with stomach cramps all day. Nobody deserves those desserts!"

Then the commentator slid into a straight news story and reported the facts: Fifty-three people, all of whom had eaten at the Republican fundraiser, had so far contacted the health department reporting symptoms of food poisoning. The majority of the afflicted had not contacted their physicians, believing their mild symptoms didn't warrant medical attention. Also, most of the afflicted, including the governor and the mayor, no longer suffered gastro-intestinal distress, but were left without energy or drive.

"That's me," Lorna said. "My batteries are dead."

"Thank goodness no one is seriously ill," Misty said. "But having both the governor and the mayor affected was a genuine stroke of bad luck."

Lorna lowered her head. "That's not the worst of it, I'm afraid."

"What do you mean?"

"Well, I tried to talk him out of it, but Raymond says he's going to sue Gene."

Horrified, Misty thought of the Andersons. She wondered if Jason Anderson was affected. Like Raymond, she was sure he'd use any excuse to get back at Gene. She could picture the Andersons and Raymond collaborating on a lawsuit and persuading others to do likewise. Her gut wrenched, as if she had food poisoning.

Misty blinked away a sudden welling of tears. Gene may be a heel, she thought, but he's a great chef and doesn't deserve to go through a legal hassle.

Her body ached with the memory of his kisses. But then she wondered how many other women had been subjected to Gene's anti-commitment lecture.

Gene rolled up the newspaper and slammed it against the deli counter. He was disgusted with the headlines that blared: "No Pearls In Those Oysters." Worse, a reporter had quoted a Democratic senator who said it wasn't the dinner that caused the illness, it was just that the Republicans had finally eaten their own words. And to top it off, the paper's political cartoonist had drawn a caricature of the governor and the mayor with clams affixed to their lips. The caption read, "Politicians Finally Clam Up."

"Suddenly everybody's a comedian," Gene cursed. With about a sixth of the diners affected with food poisoning, he wondered how he got so lucky to have both of the state's major politicians involved. He also wondered what would happen when UPI picked up the story.

Mechanically, he went about his work, mostly attending to clean-up details. He didn't expect the day to usher in any customers. He didn't bother to unlock the door, open the blinds, or turn over the CLOSED sign.

When Misty arrived, she was surprised not only to find the door locked, but a murmuring group of people gathered in front of the deli, some with noses pressed against the glass.

"When will this place open?" someone asked.

"In just a few minutes," she responded. *Unless something is wrong with Gene.* Hurriedly, she unlocked the door.

From behind the counter, Gene glanced up. "You may as well go home. We're not going to have any business today."

"Not if you don't open up, we won't. There's a crowd mingling around outside the deli now."

"Huh?"

"That's right." Misty turned the CLOSED sign

around and opened the blinds.

People streamed in.

"That's him!" a young man said, pointing to Gene.

"Yesss," a teenage girl hissed, "and he's cuter than he was on TV!"

Peering into the deli case, an elderly woman asked, "Now, young man, is this food guaranteed safe to eat?"

His ruddy complexion rapidly turning glaring crimson, Gene boomed to the crowd, "Are you people here to eat or just to gawk?"

"If you'll be seated," Misty quickly interjected, "I'll serve you."

Ignoring her offer, the group continued crowding around the counter to get a better view of Gene.

"I want to know," a massive, surly man demanded, "if you have an ax to grind with the Republican Party and if you poisoned 'em all on purpose."

"That's it," Gene boomed. "Out! All of you out! We're closed."

Threatened by Gene's menacing countenance, most of the people edged toward the door.

The surly, bushy-browed man, however, stood his ground. Boring his dark gaze into Gene's, he said, "I expect an answer."

Sensing trouble, Misty hurried to the door and opened it. "Please come back another time," she sang out.

Dawdling, the group started filing out. Gene emerged from behind the counter and joined Misty at the door. Everyone left but the surly man.

Gene sized him up. Probably never had a political

conviction in his life, Gene concluded. The man had an inch-long jagged scar in the middle of his forehead. His twisted nose appeared to have been broken–maybe more than once–and not set properly. Challenging the guy wouldn't do, Gene concluded. He's the kind of sleaze bag who'd feel honor bound to meet any physical confrontation, even if he got beaten to a pulp, which appeared to have been the case in the past. Doesn't learn from his mistakes. Gene considered his options and decided for the moment to continue the staring match, which the antagonist had started.

"I'm going to call the police," Misty announced.

"No," sleaze bag protested.

Now why didn't I think of that Gene questioned himself. The guy probably has a record a mile long.

Drawing his brows close together, bushy brows said, "I'll go, but I'll be back." He sauntered toward the door.

"Next time," Misty said in her low sensual voice, "don't forget to bring your manners."

Fearing Misty had taunted sleaze bag into protecting his dubious honor, Gene stretched a protective arm in front of Misty, forcing her to take a step backward. Insurance in case the guy tried anything as he was exiting the deli. He left without further incident. They both sighed with relief. Gene locked the door.

"Now what?" Misty asked, knowing she sounded as if she expected Gene to come up with a quick solution to staring down crowds and men who didn't want the police called.

"Like I said when you came in, you might as well go

home."

Is that what you really want? With eyes regarding Gene's shoes, she mumbled, "All right." She turned to face the door and Gene put a restraining hand on her arm. She looked fondly at the hand–it smelled of freshly ground coffee. She pictured the hand scooping coffee and idly remembered how it felt on her waist.

"Why not wait a few minutes," he said, "to be sure the crowd is disbursed." He quickly folded his arms across his chest. *Don't touch her. That's dangerous.* "Or you could go out the back door."

She sensed that his body language told her *leave.* "I'm sure they won't molest me," she responded curtly. She opened the door and heard Gene lock it behind her. The sound of it made her feel permanently locked out of his life.

A few people stood on the sidewalk outside the deli. Ignoring them, Misty went to her car and drove slowly back to her apartment.

She arrived home in time to switch on the news for an update. A spokeswoman for the health department announced that the offending organism had been determined to be a virus, and the shellfish to be the vehicle of transmission. The Washington State Health Department had been contacted and was investigating the Arctic Ocean Seafood Suppliers.

Misty switched off the news. She tried creating a new mobile, but couldn't concentrate. She usually found her work relaxing and tension relieving, but not so today. Instead of the driftwood and pieces of dried flowers filling her thoughts, Gene was there. His friendly, sexy smile and usual easy-going manner captured her imagination. *Enough!* She had to stop torturing herself this way.

She considered calling her mother, always a source of consolation and good cheer, but she didn't want to worry her parents. They'd be concerned about her job status, and she knew her perceptive mother would pick up on her disturbed emotional state as well.

Lorna strolled in, looking dejected. "I heard the latest," she lamented, "about that seafood company in Seattle, I mean."

"Maybe they're the ones Raymond should be suing."

Lorna nodded. "I'll tell him that."

"It won't matter. Raymond has a bone to pick with Gene."

"You mean he's just getting even?"

"Exactly," she said.

"We'll see. Raymond's picking me up at four. We're going to play tennis to make up for missing our game when we were sick."

"Re-charging your batteries?" Misty asked.

Lorna tilted her head, a reserved smile on her lips. "Yep. Exercise will do us both good. And how did things go with you and Gene today?"

"He closed the deli because people were streaming in to gawk, not to eat. Then he could hardly wait to get rid of me."

"I'm sure that's not true," Lorna said, a concerned frown lining her brow.

Emotion welling in her breast, Misty announced, "I'm going to shower." She decided that would help relax her.

When Misty emerged from the shower toweling her hair, Lorna informed her that Gene had just called.

"He said not to get you out of the shower, but just to tell you he's going backpacking in the foothills."

Dark eyes blazing, Misty said, "He's what?"

"Well, my goodness, he said the phone was ringing off the hook with reporters and other nosy people calling and sightseers keep tapping on the window, so there's no point in trying to run the business."

Misty inhaled sharply. "Is that it? Did he say anything else?"

"He said something about this giving you a chance to go job hunting."

"So he's that anxious to be permanently rid of me."

Hands on hips, Lorna glared at her roommate. "Well, whatever do you expect him to do under the circumstances?"

"I expect…I expect…oh, never mind." She stomped to her bedroom, slumped down on her bed, and stayed there until Raymond had collected Lorna.

So, just what did she expect? For him to be stalwart and face all adversaries? Gawking sightseers might be around the deli for days, along with sensation-seeking tabloid reporters. She guessed she couldn't blame him for wanting to leave to go backpacking, but for some inexplicable reason, she felt so alone.

At four o'clock, Misty, munching on a turkey sandwich and celery sticks, switched on the news. No new cases of food poisoning had been reported. That's one blessing, she sighed. One victim, identified as Jason Anderson, had gone to the emergency room of a local hospital, demanding to be admitted to the hospital for weight loss and dehydration. "Oh, no," Misty gasped. After consulting with the patient's private physician, the emergency room doctor declined to admit Mr. Anderson, saying he had no evidence of weight loss and his skin turgor was normal, indicating good hydration.

"The faker," Misty exclaimed aloud. He was just trying to build evidence for a lawsuit, she concluded.

In the next news segment, the CEO of the Arctic Ocean Seafood Suppliers in Seattle was interviewed live.

"We've sold small amounts of seafood to Mr. Gene Haynes of Sacramento in the past," the CEO said, "but never a large order."

Misty's jaw dropped and her eyes widened.

"So you deny that the seafood implicated in the recent food poisoning cases came from your company?" the interviewer asked.

"Absolutely. We've contacted our lawyers to determine how to proceed with Mr. Haynes' false accusation."

"Liar," Misty shouted at the CEO. "I have the receipt with your company's name on it."

She grabbed a windbreaker and her purse. Ponytail flapping, she raced down the stairs to her car.

When Misty drove up to the deli, she was disgusted to find several people attempting to peer through the window with its closed blinds. All parking spots were taken. She parked in front of a water hydrant, not caring if she were ticketed. Locating her key to the deli, she stepped out of her car, passed the gawkers without glancing at them, and unlocked the door.

"Hey, when are you opening?" someone asked.

"Not for several days," she responded.

She stepped into the deli, closed the door, and went directly to the file cabinet where she kept all the records pertaining to the banquet. Startled to hear the door opening, she whirled around to see Sam entering. Her heart jumped.

"You need to lock the door to keep 'em out," he said. He slid the dead bolt in place.

Unnerved, she asked, "What are you doing here?"

"Heard about all the trouble. Thought I'd stop by to see if I could help."

Rummaging through the file, she responded, "The company you drive for denies selling the seafood to Gene."

"Yeah. I heard that on the news."

"But I have the receipt in here." She located the folder and extracted the paper. "Here it is."

"Give it to me," San directed. "I'll take care of it."

She didn't like the demanding undertone in his voice. She looked up sharply to see him, hand outstretched, advancing toward her.

Heart pounding, she folded the receipt and held it tightly in one hand. "I'll see to it that Gene gets this."

His jaw tensed and his lower lip twitched. "I said I'll take care of it. I'll clear Gene's name. Now hand it over."

Confused thoughts racing through her head, Misty couldn't fathom why Sam was behaving this way. Instinct told her not to relinquish the receipt.

"I prefer to take care of it myself," she said, drawing herself to her full height and staring directly into Sam's narrowing eyes.

He stepped closer to her. In less than a second he could grab her, she reasoned. He could easily overpower her, even crush her flat with his pendulous abdomen. Realizing there was no way she could get by him to the locked door, she suddenly side-stepped, slipping behind the counter and raced to the front window. She jerked the cord that raised the blinds. She smiled and waved at the gawkers. Sam reached her, grabbing her right arm.

She transferred the receipt to her left hand and stuffed it down her bra. "Let me go," she screamed.

Sam looked at her, then at the potential witnesses outside. He released her. "Sure. Don't get excited. Just thought I could handle it better than you."

Misty pushed the dead bolt and opened the door.

"What's happening in there?" one of the spectators asked.

Ignoring the questioner, Misty stared hard at Sam. She swept her arm across the threshold. "After you," she said.

Firm lipped, he hesitated, then walked past her.

For a moment, Misty closed her eyes and released a tense sigh. She crossed the threshold, locked the door, and went to her car. Darn. She had left her purse inside. Too bad. She'd have to do without it. She had her keys and that's all she needed.

She fired the engine and checked the gas gauge. Three-quarters full. She made a U-turn and headed for Interstate 80 East. Her destination was Miners' Ravine Trailhead. Gene had a head start, but she reasoned he wouldn't have been in a hurry, and since she wasn't loaded with a pack, her chances of catching up with him were good.

She forced herself to take a deep, restorative breath to calm and relax her for what may lie ahead, then put the car in cruise control so she couldn't exceed the speed limit by more than a few miles. It wouldn't do to be stopped for speeding, especially since her driver's license was in her purse back at the deli.

In about an hour, she was well out of the oak-filled valley and into the pine-forested, undulating foothills of the Sierra. She moved to the right lane.

When she exited the freeway, she turned left. Soon she found herself on the narrow, twisting road that she and Gene had traveled together. The road seemed more precipitous than when she was with Gene, and not at all like downhill skiing as he had said. Grateful for her compact car, she concentrated on her mission. She turned on her headlights just in case a car was coming from the other direction. In her rear-view mirror, she thought she detected a vehicle behind her. Strange. This isn't exactly a well-traveled road, she mused.

It seemed like hours later, but Misty knew it had been only a matter of minutes when spotted Gene's van at the trailhead. She pulled up alongside it and parked. The heavy, pine-laden air was cooler than in the valley. She grabbed her windbreaker, shoved her arms into it, and locked her car.

Another car emerged from the final twist in the road. Her startled, unbelieving eyes told her that the driver was Sam! Misty bounded toward the trail and began descending the sharp-edged switchbacks. They had seemed more rounded and friendly when she and Gene hiked down them.

"Hey, I just want to talk to you!" she heard Sam call.

Ignoring him, she deftly continued her descent into Miners' Ravine Canyon. Sam called for her again. Panicked, she wondered what would happen if he caught up with her. At best, he'd force her to give him the receipt. She pictured him roughly extracting the receipt from her bra. She shuddered. But why was he so set on having the receipt? She didn't have time to try to reason that out. She tried not to think of the worst possible scenario if Sam overtook her. He was capable of brutalizing her; she had seen cruelty in his eyes at the deli. She simply couldn't let him catch her. How was she to prevent it?

Approaching the next switchback, Misty noted a clump of manzanita shrubs skirting a low rock formation about fifty feet down the embankment. Without hesitation, she half walked, half slid down to the bushes. Lying flat on the ground behind the rocks, she knew she was concealed from the view of anyone on the trail. Even so, she not only could feel her heart beating, she could hear it, too. She couldn't breathe fast enough to keep up with it.

As she heard Sam approach in his heavy boots, she inhaled deeply and held her breath, fearing he would detect the sound of her respirations. He called to her again, assuring her he only wanted to "talk."

She ventured a cautious glance through a manzanita bush and saw Sam's back disappearing around the next switchback. She startled at the sight of a snub-nosed revolver hooked under his belt.

How long would it be before he realized I tricked him she wondered. She counted to five to be certain he was out of earshot of her next move.

Misty looked with apprehension at the long, steep granite embankment, but hesitated only a moment before starting to schuss down the grade in a sitting position. Crab-like, she used her hands and feet to scoot on her bottom. Impeded by prickly bushes and assorted rocks, she soon felt burned and bruised. Rounding one bush, the steep granite propelled her downward like a child on a playground slide. She grasped frantically at every passing branch. A gap appeared in the granite ahead. She saw no way to avoid it.

Suddenly she was suspended in space, then slammed into a stubby manzanita bush. Stunned, she lay quietly. Glancing up at the ridge she'd tumbled off, she determined she had free fallen about three feet. She waited for pain to tell her which limbs she'd broken, but none arrived. Just her skin was uncomfortable, excoriated as if burned. Okay, move, she ordered herself. You've got to see if everything works. Gingerly, she moved her arms, then her legs. As she sat up, her bottom sank further into the bush. Wrestling with the branches, she untangled herself, stood, then again assumed a squatting position, and scooted the rest of the way down.

Glancing up to the trail, Misty's worst fear was realized. Sam was staring directly at her. *At least I'm out of range of his handgun.* With his girth, he could slide down that bank in seconds. She decided his poor physical shape would prevent that. She bounded toward the cover of the trees, then slowed down. She could easily trip or twist an ankle on this rock-strewn terrain.

She finally reached the river at a shallow spot where rocks had been placed in strategic positions for stepping-stones. She decided to cross. It wasn't a log like she and Gene had used to cross, but it would get her on the opposite side. She slipped once, but the water at that spot was only knee deep. *At least now I am on the opposite side of the river from Sam.*

She began picking her way more carefully. Gene and Dave's favorite camping spot is on this side, she knew. But how far down?

Lengthening shadows created eerie patterns, telling her it wouldn't be long before sunset. How would she find Gene before dark she worried, not allowing the panic in her stomach to rise. In her haste to leave the deli, she hadn't even considered the possibility of not finding him.

A full bladder made walking increasingly more difficult. Misty glanced around for a bush to hide behind, then scoffed at herself as if it mattered if anyone saw her. She hoped someone would. She unzipped her jeans, squatted, relieved herself, and fastened. Picking up her pace, she reasoned that she had to concentrate on increasing the distance between herself and Sam.

The western sky blushed with a lavish show of color; darkness was rapidly approaching. She wondered what Gene saw when he looked at a sky like this. Was it all one color?

She'd soon need a flashlight, but of course she didn't have one. Using one would be foolish anyway, she reasoned, as it would enable Sam to spot her from a distance. She hoped he'd be reluctant to use one for the same reason.

A hesitant moon rose, but was of no help in lighting her way because of the denseness of the forest. She sniffed the air, hoping to catch the scent of a campfire, or perhaps fish frying or coffee brewing. Nothing.

She'd have to find a spot to land until morning. She comforted herself with the knowledge that even if she didn't find Gene, she was bound to come across other backpackers or fishermen the next day. The prospect of a long, cold night loomed threateningly ahead. Even if he was a cad, she longed for the warmth and protection of Gene's strong arms.

Although darkness threatened, she decided to go a few more yards. She edged along, using the trees as guides.

During the day, pines were not only beautiful, but symmetrical and majestic as they thrust toward the sky. But their beauty turned ugly with the night, their bark menacing, threatening to tear her abraded skin. The haunting sounds of the forest enchanted her during the day–the chatter of chipmunks, the chirping of birds, the breezes whistling through pine needles, creating natural wind chimes. Now, in the darkness, the sounds were foreign and frightening. Even the odor of the forest was odd and oppressive. She stifled a sob.

Feeling her way along a tree, she reached out for another trunk, but touched only air. She took one hesitant step forward. Her foot stubbed the roots of a tree that clung to the side of a knoll. She struggled to gain her footing, but felt herself toppling over. She hit the ground on her side and rolled several feet down the bank, landing flat on her back.

Dazed, Misty gazed at sparkling diamonds in a deep blue pendant sky. Then a spotlight shone directly in her face.

Chapter 10

"What the hell!"

The deep voice sounded vaguely familiar, but in her hazy state, Misty couldn't connect it with a face. Nevertheless, the instinct for self-preservation took hold and she hissed, "Turn out the light."

The light stayed on as the shadowy figure stepped to her side, hunkered down on his haunches, and said, "Misty–are you okay? Do you hurt any place?"

Gene. Of course. The voice belonged to Gene.

"I think I'm okay," she murmured. "I'm too stunned to hurt anywhere." She lifted her hand to her face to shield her eyes from the light. "Turn the flashlight off. Sam is after me."

He grazed the light over her body and detected no blood or twisted limbs, so he switched the light off. "What do you mean Sam is after you?"

Through a fog, she said, "Sam's following me. He's after the receipt."

"Whoa! What receipt? Wait–never mind. Let's check you over first to see if you've done any damage."

Good. She didn't have the energy to relate the whole story. Her mind and body were heavy, immovable objects, like a boulder half-sunken into the earth.

Gene cautiously guided his hands to the back of her neck and gently pressed on her vertebrae. "Does that hurt?"

"No. It feels wonderful."

He placed his hands on either side of her ribs and pressed inward. "Does that hurt?" he asked.

"No." Don't stop, she wanted to add.

Next, he checked her arms, then her legs. She had no pain and she was able to move each limb. He assumed her bones were intact. "Your feet and lower legs are wet."

"I stepped into the river. Accident." She hoped he wasn't finished examining her.

"Why such flimsy tennis shoes?" he asked.

"Didn't have time to change. No time," she said again, confirming Gene's suspicion that she wasn't all there, yet.

He shook his head, bemused by her answers, and astounded by her presence. He'd have to sort all that out later. Right now, he needed to take her wet things off and get her settled in a bedroll.

"Can you sit up?" he asked.

She struggled to force her body out of the ground. "I need a fulcrum," she moaned. In spite of himself, he grinned. She managed to sit without assistance.

"Where's your backpack?"

"I didn't bring one. Didn't have time."

He cursed softly. What the hell could she have been thinking? If she hadn't stumbled across him, she would have spent the night shivering in the woods. No sense in bringing that up now. Eventually, the full story would come out. And he sensed he wouldn't like it.

"Let me help you stand. My campsite is just a few yards away."

"On level ground, I hope."

"Right." He squatted in front of her. "Put your arms around my neck." She complied like an obedient child. He wrapped his arms around her and lifted her to a standing position.

"I'm going to turn on the flashlight just long enough to get us over there where my pack and bag are. We don't need any more falls." Still holding her with one arm, he picked up the flashlight and switched it on.

Misty gingerly stepped forward and gratefully realized all her parts worked.

When they reached his campsite, he had her sit on the ground. "Take the light," he directed, gesturing to his right, "and shine it over here."

Numb from head to toe, Misty felt paralyzed, barely able to follow his directions. In her stuporous state, she stared without sight as Gene unzipped the sleeping bag.

"We can sleep on the ground cover, under the bag. I don't suppose you brought any food."

"No."

"Hungry?"

"No." Staring at the ground cover, she crawled to it, then collapsed. She was more exhausted–physically and emotionally–than she could ever remember being. She felt like a rung-out sponge.

She was only vaguely aware of her shoes and socks being removed. Then her jeans were unsnapped.

"Lift your hips," Gene directed.

She complied, then felt her jeans being tugged over her bottom. Gene was removing her pants and she was listlessly letting him do it. She was too tired to care. She heard him shake them out. Then strong, efficient fingers pulled woolen socks over her feet.

"That's grand," she said.

Gene covered her with the sleeping bag and switched off the light.

"Misty, before you go to sleep, you've got to tell me what you're doing here."

He was right. She had to tell him. To warn him about Sam. Laboriously, she strained to remember.

"The four o'clock news," she began. "The seafood company denied selling any large quantity of shellfish to you. I went to the deli to get the receipt. Sam was there. He ordered me to give him the receipt. I didn't. I got away. Wanted to find you. He followed me. He has a gun."

Bewildered by her story, Gene shook his head, wondering what the devil Sam was up to. But for now, Misty needed quiet and rest. "Okay. That's enough. We'll talk more in the morning." He tucked the edge of the sleeping bag under her and laid down beside her, acutely aware of her state of undress. What kind of lecherous fool am I, he wondered, having sexual notions about a woman who's obviously exhausted after a terrifying experience?

Every one of Misty's muscles hurt. Her head was spinning. Mercifully, she drifted off into a troubled sleep. In her dreams, she was Snow White running through the woods. The forest, once kind and nurturing, turned threatening and foreboding. Wind whipped and swirled about her as if she were in a tornado. Distorted tree branches transformed into gnarly fingers, writhing to bend and scratch her. The raccoons and squirrels, formerly cartoon cute and friendly, ran about her, hissing and growling. Owls and bats hovered over her, screeching raucously. Darkness enveloped her.

A large man with a pendulous abdomen chased her. He was closing the distance between them. The harder she tried to move her legs, the slower they seemed to go. Her pursuer drew near–he reached out a hand to grab her.

Misty sat straight up, gasping for air and clutching at her throat. Dizzy and confused, her mind struggled for reality.

"You're okay," a deep comforting voice said. A firm, gentle arm circled her shoulders.

Gene. Yes, as long as he was next to her, everything would be okay.

"You're all right, Misty. You're safe now," he continued in a calm, soothing tone. "Here, lie back down." With her head resting on his arm, he guided her until she was once again resting on the ground cover. She lay very still. He drew her close to him and reached around her to be sure her back was well covered by the sleeping bag. He touched his lips to her forehead. Her breathing calmed.

Damn. Sure he left Sacramento to get away from the harassment of the sightseers and sensation seekers, but he also left to be away from Misty. He needed time to sort out his feelings about her. But now, here she was, lying next to him, cradled in his arms. Thank God. He loved having her there. What he had discovered in those few hours of contemplation away from her was that he needed her. Oh, not just to work in the deli or to help with catering, and not just to warm his bed. He needed her in order to feel whole. Whenever he was separated from her he yearned for her, and the mere sight of her filled an aching void.

So this was love. The thought didn't surprise him: he loved her.

She stirred in her sleep. He tightened his arms around her and massaged her back until she relaxed.

Considering their options, Gene thought they could go back the way they came and risk encountering Sam, or they could go forward and Sam might follow them. *Not much of a choice.* However, he thought it would be less likely that Sam would follow them if they went on. He stayed awake most of the night, short bursts of sleep occasionally overtaking him. He needed to be alert in case Sam was nearby.

With strong arms safely housing her, Misty escaped into a deep sleep. It seemed only minutes later when she was aware of a gun pressing into her head.

She decided to lie very still. If she played dead,

maybe Sam would go away. No, he'll never go away, she reasoned, until he gets what he wants. Would he tear her bra off to get it? Why didn't he speak? Gradually, she awakened more fully to the realization that the 'gun' was her ponytail pressing into the back of her head. She opened her eyes and was barely able to see the outline of Gene's wonderful face in front of her. She felt his breath whisper over her cheek.

"Are you awake?" she whispered.

"Yes. Would you mind moving your head? Your pony tail is killing my arm."

"Sorry," she responded, "but it's better than a gun."

"Huh?"

"Nothing. Just a dream." Relaxed in his embrace, she inhaled deeply, a mixture of his masculine scent and the frosty mountain air tickling her nostrils. "It'll be light soon, won't it?"

"Yes. We'd better be on our way."

She willed him to kiss her good morning. He didn't. "But Sam is between us and our cars," she said.

Gene sat up. "I know. So we'll continue downstream. Are you up to it?"

She knew she had to be up to it. "Everything seems to be in working order."

"I don't see much danger in Sam catching up with us, he's so overweight and out of shape."

"I wouldn't count on that. He had a determined gleam in his eye when he demanded I give him the receipt."

"By the way, where is the receipt?"

"Uh...in a safe place."

"Where?"

"In my bra."

He shook his head, thinking of what else was in her bra. "Your jeans and tennis shoes are still damp." He handed them to her.

She slid her legs in her pants. "At least I have nice dry socks."

"Too big. You'll have to stuff them inside your shoes." He hesitated, then the fear he'd been feeling for her safety erupted. "What the hell possessed you to come into the woods alone and so totally unprepared?"

"I just wanted to find you," she squeaked.

Oh, lord, did he hear a sob in her throat? He heaved a sigh. *Well, they had to make the best of it now.* Then something she had said the night before struck him. "The five o'clock news? If you saw the five o'clock news, then went to the deli, how could you possibly have made it down here before dark?"

She hesitated, considering her options. The truth or a lie? She wanted to lie, but didn't know a convincing fib to tell. A helicopter brought her? No, that wouldn't do at all. She braced herself for an onslaught of cursing.

"I skipped the switchbacks and scooted on my bottom down to the river."

His jaw dropped. He wanted to shake her until her teeth rattled. He wanted to pull her over his knee and spank her. He wanted to crush her to him and thank heaven she was safe. At any rate, he didn't want to think about it further. He closed his mouth.

"Give me some light," he directed, handing her the flashlight, "so I can get my pack down."

Puzzled at his lack of response, she wondered if he had heard her confession. She shone the light between two trees where he had strung his pack to keep it away from hungry animals. He fished in his pack and pulled out a sweatshirt. "Here–put this on. You'll freeze in that flimsy windbreaker."

"Thanks." She pulled it over her head, then wrestled with her damp shoes while he stuffed the sleeping bag in its cover. Together, they folded the ground cover.

"Sore this morning?" he asked.

"A little," she fibbed. Actually, she ached all over. "I'm mostly thirsty."

He handed her his canteen then hoisted his pack on his back.

She drank greedily. "Let me at least carry this." She slung the canteen strap over her shoulder.

Taking the lead, Gene moved ahead cautiously in the early morning light. He headed downstream, parallel with the river, but far enough away to remain in the cover of the trees.

Is it possible Sam is ahead of us, Misty worried? No, not likely. But her impetuous actions had put Gene as well as herself in jeopardy. Logically, she should have gone to the police. It wasn't like her to act without thinking. But then she hadn't been thinking well of late.

As the day lightened, Gene picked up the pace. They had hiked for over two hours when he stopped. "Let's take a break. I'm going to the john." He disappeared behind a large boulder. Misty needed to relieve herself, too. She found a shielding oak. When she emerged, Gene handed her a package of gorp.

"Don't think I should spend the time to fix us a proper meal, so here's breakfast on the run."

She glanced at his bulging backpack. "Couldn't I carry some things in your pack? It looks like you have an awful lot of stuff."

"I'm okay. You need to keep both hands free for balance."

They set out again, munching as they walked. She liked being behind him, watching him move. He seemed so at home in the woods, moving easily, as if he were a bear who lived there.

"How soon before we reach civilization?" Misty asked.

"Not for another day."

She gasped. "You mean we'll be spending another night in the woods?"

"Afraid so. With any luck we'll meet up with other backpackers. Safety in numbers."

Gene stopped in front of a granite embankment that snaked out at the bottom, touching the river. When he'd reached this point previously, he had skirted the granite, wading in the river to get around it. But if he and Misty did that, Sam was likely to spot them even from a long distance.

"I think we should climb it," he mused, more to himself than to Misty. "From the rear where it's not so steep."

Misty gulped. She had never done any kind of rock climbing. And with every muscle aching, now didn't seem to be the time to learn.

"We'll have a good view up there, too," he mumbled. He shrugged his shoulders, settling his pack, then marched toward the rear of the granite outcropping.

Misty scrambled to keep up with him.

He turned and read anxiety on her face. "Look," he said reassuringly, "it isn't very steep on this side. Just watch where I put my feet, then you do the same."

She tried to relax and radiate a confidence she didn't fee. "I'll try. I mean, yes, I'll do it."

"Anyone who can slide down that granite mountain can climb this little hill," he added.

So, he had heard her confession. He must have been too aghast to respond. "I'm game," she said.

Misty followed in Gene's footsteps, pleased she was able to keep up with him in spite of her aching body. Within half an hour, Gene had reached the top. He grasped Misty's arm and hauled her up, then laid on his back to catch his breath. Misty joined him, looking up to watch horizontal gray clouds scuttle across an azure sky.

Gene rose and walked to the edge of the granite outcropping. Cautiously, Misty followed. A lightning bolt of horror struck her.

"Oh, no! It's Sam!"

Their paunchy adversary was trudging on the other side of the river, almost directly across from them.

"Get down," Gene ordered.

Too late. Sam caught sight of them, opening his

mouth as if to shout, but the bellow of the river drowned him out.

They scurried back, out of sight of Sam. Swell idea to climb this damn rock, Gene thought. Had a great view all right. Unfortunately, so did Sam.

"He's really pretty far away from us, isn't he?" Misty asked hopefully.

"Yeah. He'll have to cross the river to get near us." He hoped his calm voice reassured her. "Now let's get off this granite and back into the woods."

They clamored down and continued hiking in the clearest part of the forest. Gene avoided breaking foliage; he didn't want to leave a trail to follow.

"Sam must be awfully hungry by now," Misty said.

"Not likely. He always has his pockets full of candy. Wants to be sure he doesn't experience a single pang of hunger."

"Why do you suppose he's so intent on getting the receipt?"

Gene had been mulling that one over. "Can't figure it out. He must not have gotten the seafood from the Arctic Ocean Company. Maybe he forged the receipt and wants to destroy the evidence."

Misty agreed. "That's the only thing that seems to make sense."

They continued hiking, swiftly and silently. Misty's feet hurt. She felt every rock and twig through her tennis shoes. Gene's thick socks provided some cushion, but they were too big and they scrunched up uncomfortably inside her shoes. She was grateful when Gene halted, declaring a lunch break. She sat on the ground and elevated her feet on a boulder. Glancing up at the sky, she saw more gray than blue.

"I hope the clouds hold on to their moisture," she said.

Gene removed his pack and rummaged around inside for suitable finger foods. He located beef jerky, cheese, crackers, and dried fruit. They ate sparingly and once again were on their way.

"Aren't you surprised we haven't met anyone else?" Misty asked.

"It's a weekday. A little early in the season, too."

Later, she asked, "Are those pine needles falling or is sprinkling?"

Noting the darkening skies, he answered, "Afraid it's sprinkling."

Visibility worsened, but they trudged ahead.

"Darn it," Misty exclaimed.

Gene turned to face her. "What's the matter?"

"I twisted my ankle over a rock. It's nothing. Really. Let's keep going."

They didn't have much choice, Gene mused. He continued leading, looking along the way for suitable shelter for the night. The sky colored itself from gray to black. The sprinkles turned into a steady drizzle.

"This way," Gene said, directing Misty off to the right. "There are some overhanging rocks over there."

They wended their way around bushes and trees and found some dry ground under a granite shelf.

"It's not a cave," Gene commented, "but at least we

have a roof." *Lord. He was going to have to spend another night lying beside her.*

Their bed for the night would be on a slant but they decided that was the best they could do. They smoothed out an area for the ground cover and laid it down.

Gratefully, Misty sank to her knees. "It was thoughtful of you to have a padded ground cover. Almost as if you were expecting company." She removed her sweatshirt and her shoes, grimacing when she touched her tender ankle. Ironic, she thought. I fall twice and don't do any damage to myself, but stumble over a rock and sprain my ankle. She undid her ponytail.

"I like to rough it in comfort." He opened the sleeping bag and covered her. When he lay down beside her, she rolled on her side to face him, snuggling close. He took a deep breath and slipped an arm under her neck to pillow her head. He kept his other hand on his thigh. "Tell me about sliding down the mountain," he said.

"I found out it's difficult to slide on granite. It's kind of sticky. Anyway, I was so fixed on getting away from Sam that I didn't notice much until I fell off a ledge."

He groaned, not sure he wanted to hear more.

"The fall startled me into being more careful. I just scooted on my bottom the rest of the way."

"And then you fell into my camp. You must be thoroughly bruised all over."

"It does kind of feel that way."

He stroked her back, hoping to quiet and relax her.

She closed her eyes, reveling in the feel of his fingers working their magic on her tired, aching muscles. "Last night the sky was awash with color at sunset," she murmured. "I wondered what you saw when you looked at it."

He tensed. "I saw the sunset."

She opened her eyes to look at him. "I mean—now don't get upset, but I know you're colorblind."

He stopped stroking her back. "I am not blind to color. I have a color-vision deficiency."

"What's the difference?"

He sighed. "Semantics, mostly. But I do see more than black and white."

"I've just wondered why you're so sensitive about it. Has it caused you a lot of pain over the years?"

For the first time he could remember, Gene didn't feel threatened talking about his colorblindness. He felt he could trust her, that she wouldn't belittle the problem. She'd take it seriously and wouldn't make a joke out of it.

"It's like something is missing," he explained. "Like you're not whole."

She ran her hand over the stubble on his face. "I've never known a more whole human being."

He captured her hand and kissed the palm. "Go to sleep."

"I can't. You're too close."

"I'll move over."

"You won't be able to move far enough."

"You have to go to sleep. We have another long day tomorrow."

Forgetting her anger, she kissed his neck.

"Cut it out."

"Just kiss me good night."

"Misty, in case you've forgotten, a guy with a gun is chasing us."

"I know. If he catches up with us, this may be our last night together."

Lord. What an exasperating female. "Don't get theatrical on me. We need a good rest."

She thought that even if they emerged from this experience unscathed, this would indeed be their last night together. They'd each be going their separate ways. She couldn't stay at the deli, loving him, but not having that love returned. She needed the memory of this night for warmth and comfort in the unending void that stretched ahead of her.

"One kiss," she whispered.

"Misty," Gene breathed. With a finger under her chin, he tilted her head back and brushed his lips against hers.

"That was just a tease," she complained.

He circled her with his arms, crushing her to him while covering her mouth with his. He felt, then heard paper crackle. "What's that?"

She reached into her bra and extracted the receipt. "Well, it was safe from Sam," she said.

"I wouldn't be so sure about that." He shoved the receipt into his back pocket, then flipped over, turning his back to her.

"It's stopped raining," Misty whispered. "Look—a star."

She wasn't sure Gene had heard her. His breathing

was deep and rhythmic, the sonorous sound of sleep.

A second star appeared. And then a third. Finally, she could see part of the moon above the dark clouds. Her lids closed and she fell asleep to the contralto call of distant coyotes.

Chapter 11

Misty awakened to the gentle rays of the eastern sun filtering through the pines. Gently, she tapped Gene. "It's light outside."

He rolled over to his back, a bent arm covering his eyes.

She grasped his shoulder and shook. "Wake up," she said softly

"Huh?" He flung his arm away from his eyes, then raised his lids. "Oh, hell! How did we sleep so long?" He jumped up, and shoved his shirttail into his jeans. Viciously, he began stuffing the sleeping bag into its cover. "We should have been out of here an hour ago. Hell, we may as well run up a flag that'll show Sam the way."

Misty was too engrossed with trying to get her shoes on to respond. The left shoe slipped on easily, but her right ankle was swollen, stiff, and sore. Bending her ankle to put the shoe on caused more discomfort than she wanted to reveal to the furious man standing near her.

She struggled to her feet and began folding the

ground cover. Gene snatched it away from her and finished the job. "Let's get the hell out of here."

They scrambled down from their rock shelter and set out. Misty was glad to follow in Gene's wake so he wouldn't see her limping. No doubt he'd go from furious to enraged at her clumsiness. She only hoped she could keep up with his long strides.

An hour later, Misty found herself skipping occasionally on her left foot in order to avoid putting weight on her right ankle.

Perturbed with the hopping sounds, Gene stopped, then turned to face her. "What the hell are you doing?"

She halted. Hands on hips, dark eyes flashing, she retorted, "Will you stop swearing at me!"

His anger vanished. His voice softened. "Tell me why you're hopping."

"I'm not hopping. I'm skipping."

Clenching his teeth, he said, "Okay. Skipping. Why?"

"My ankle's swollen."

"Why the h–why didn't you say something? I've got an elastic bandage in my pack." She didn't answer his question, but she didn't have to. He knew why she hadn't complained. She was afraid he'd get angrier. He sighed audibly.

"Better sit down," he directed. "Get the shoe and sock off." He shrugged out of his pack and located the elastic bandage. He applied a figure eight bandage over the foot and ankle, rolled his sock over it, then together they managed to squeeze her foot back into her canvas shoe. It gaped open. There was no way they could tie the lace. "It'll have to do." He shook his head. "It should be raised with ice on it."

"A little punishment won't hurt it." She stood and put weight on the foot, suppressing a grimace. "The bandage does help. Let's go."

Gene hated to do it, but thinking of Misty's ankle, he slowed his pace. As best he could, he stayed away from obstacles that could trip her up again. Damn. Why didn't she at least put her hiking boots on before rushing out into the woods?

They stopped for a bladder break, then grabbed some food they could munch while hiking.

"There's hardly a swallow of water left," Misty said, a concerned edge to her voice.

"I've got a filter," Gene responded, "so we can use river water if we need to."

"I wonder what Sam's drinking."

"River water loaded with Giardia, I hope. Belly pain and diarrhea would serve him right after the seafood he delivered to me." He took a generous bite of jerky. "How's the ankle?"

"It's okay," she lied. She glanced above the conifers to see a graying sky. "Looks like we might be in for some more rain. How much longer till we reach civilization?"

"A few more miles downstream, then we'll cross the river."

"Is there a bridge?"

"A natural bridge of rocks."

Misty tensed, thinking of balancing on rocks with her

unsteady, painful ankle. "And there'll be people on the other side?"

Gene hesitated, not wanting to give her false encouragement, but not wanting to lie to her, either. "Maybe not," he answered, "but there's a trail that leads to people."

She silently moaned. Afraid of the next answer, she asked, "How long is the trail?"

"Not sure. When Dave and I did this hike, we returned on the other side of the river." Then he quickly added, "But of course the trail will get us to civilization sooner."

When they stopped for a short break mid-afternoon, Misty sat and elevated her foot.

Gene lightly ran his hand over the bandaged ankle.

"It's okay," she said.

Tough lady. Reluctantly, he rose, then helped her stand. They set out once again.

As shadows lengthened, they reached the natural bridge of rocks and gingerly began crossing the river. Grasping Misty's hand to steady her, Gene led the way.

Misty tried to relax, knowing if she tensed she'd be more likely to lose her footing. The rocks were actually boulders. If her ankle were only normal, she thought, she'd have no difficulty at all.

Midway across, she glanced back. Gene felt her stiffen and heard a foreign, animal sound emanate from deep within her throat.

"What's wrong?" he shouted, in order to be heard above the rushing sounds of the river.

"It's Sam!"

Gene turned to see Sam jump on the first rock in the natural bridge. He held a gun in his right hand, his left hand cupped under his right wrist to hold it steady. The gun was pointing directly at them.

"Good God." Gene hooked his wrists under Misty's arms, half lifting, half dragging her. "Move in front of me," he ordered. He got her on the boulder with him, encouraging her to go forward when he felt a sudden, sharp pain in his right calf. His right foot slipped off the rock, plunging his leg into the swiftly running river water. He hadn't heard the shot, the roar of the river masking the sound.

Horror-stricken, Misty saw blood mingling with the water. "Step up, Gene." She tugged at him. "Come on–we have to get to the shelter of the trees."

"Go on without me."

"No! I won't leave without you."

Stubborn, foolish female. He struggled to regain his footing.

Misty again looked at Sam who now stood on the second boulder, gun again leveled at them. She heard a shrill, piercing scream that she didn't recognize as her own.

The next bullet hit Gene's backpack, again throwing him off balance. Both legs were now in the water up to his crotch. Misty was grateful to see the recoil had also upended Sam who now stood waist-deep in the river.

"Hurry," Misty yelled, "before he has a chance to get off another shot." She took a step forward on her injured ankle; her foot slipped on the wet granite and she plunged into the frigid water next to Gene. He grasped her around the waist to steady her. Bracing their arms on the rocks, the pair waded the rest of the way across.

Between the cold water and the fright, Misty's ankle no longer hurt. The cold surely would stop Gene's bleeding, she hoped.

Dragging themselves out of the river, they scrambled up the steep bank and raced for the cover of the trees and boulders.

Gene removed his backpack and extracted the flashlight. "I can't walk any more, Misty. My leg gives out." He pointed off to their left. "There's the trail. Take the flashlight and go."

"No! I can't leave you to the mercy of that monster."

"I'll hide. Look–there's a boulder that's plenty big enough. Sam will think we both took the trail and will be after you. Hurry!"

Frantic, Misty threw her arms around his neck and kissed him.

He unwound her arms, turned her around, and slapped her on her bottom. "Now go! Step lively, but carefully."

She turned once at the trailhead to satisfy herself that Gene was concealing himself as he said, then she took off at as fast a clip as her stiff, swollen ankle would allow.

Gene watched her disappear into the forest. "Be careful," he whispered, his chest tightening with fear.

His whole leg ached, but that was okay. The pain would keep him alert, watching and listening for Sam.

Dinner for Two

Steely clouds overhead released a fine drizzle. Darkness was fast approaching.

Gene heard splashing noises. Sam was wading out of the river. Then he was scrambling up the bank. All of Gene's muscles went taut, ready for action. Quick steps and heavy rapid breathing warned him of Sam's approach. Crouching, Gene peered out from behind his rock wall. In the dim light, he could clearly see Sam's outline.

Sam turned on his flashlight and examined the ground. Gene trembled with rage when he realized Sam saw Misty's footprints in the soft earth. Sam aimed his flashlight beam toward the trail.

Don't cry, Misty ordered herself. You won't be able to see. You have to keep your eyes clear and your wits about you. You have to stay ahead of Sam and get help for Gene.

Her body and mind calmed and became one. She was conscious only of putting one foot in front of the other. Like an animal operating on the instinct of self-preservation, she pressed forward, ignoring the pain in her ankle. It was only pain. She could deal with it.

The drizzle stopped, but darkness forced her to turn on the flashlight. The moon peeked through the clouds, offering a minuscule shard of light to help her on her way.

The well-traveled trail followed close to the river, reassuring her that she wouldn't get lost in the woods. Her feet sloshed in her saturated tennis shoes. The saturated bandage on her ankle was heavy, slowing her pace.

A noise up ahead caused her to hesitate. She tensed with fear for the first time since leaving Gene. Shining the flashlight toward the sound, she saw two skunks waddling away from the river. She respectfully gave them a wide berth.

The feeling of fear awakened her other senses. She shivered from the cold and suddenly felt bone weary. Pain shot up her leg every time her right foot hit the ground. She considered yelling for help, but reasoned that Sam might hear her.

How far have I come? A mile? Two miles? She lost all sense of time and distance. Feeling like a turtle, she plodded ahead while looking down and watching her feet move. She had to pick up speed. Sam might overtake her. She decided to look forward, toward the end of the flashlight beam. Perhaps she wouldn't be as conscious of her cold, aching feet that way.

She squinted, straining to peer ahead in the darkness. Was that a light up ahead, or was it like a mirage in the desert? An extra surge of adrenaline helped speed her pace. It was a light! She continued her quickened pace, calling out, "Help! Can someone hear me?"

No answer. She covered a few more feet before yelling again. This time she got a response. A man's voice answered: "Yes. We can hear you. Are you hurt?"

We. There was more than one person. Thank heaven. "I'm okay, but I need help."

Two flashlights shone her way as she dragged her body forward. Just a few more feet, she promised herself, then you can rest.

She stumbled over a rock and felt herself pitch forward. Strong arms caught her.

"Steady, now," a voice said. An arm went solidly around her back to support her. Magically, another arm went around her other side; she was lifted until her toes barely touched the ground. She felt like a ballet dancer being supported by a harness dangling from a ceiling.

Two men carried her to their camp and deposited her inside a tent where her feckless knees sunk to the ground.

"Why, you poor dear, whatever happened?" A large, buxom woman with short, salt and pepper hair stood over her. Misty almost managed a smile.

"Now, Ma, she doesn't want to gab," said her first rescuer, whom she guessed to be the woman's husband. Her second rescuer was a younger, slimmer version of the first.

"Yes," Misty protested. "I have to talk. My friend has been shot. He's back–" she waved in the general direction of the trail "–probably a couple of miles. I can't be sure. But he needs help. And the man who shot him might still be after me." She drew a deep breath. "I hope I haven't put you all in any danger."

"If he shows up here, he'll be looking down the barrels of three rifles–mine and my two sons'."

Misty sighed with relief. "Can you call for an ambulance?"

"We'll get on the CB and have help down here quick as a wink," the woman said.

"Oh, thank you." Tears of relief spilled over Misty's lids, cascading down her cheeks.

211

A hand patted her head. The woman said, "Everything's going to be all right now, sweetie. My name's Anna, honey. That's my husband, John, who's on the CB, and those two tall, lanky guys are our sons, Matthew and Michael. Michael and John carried you here. Now you just get all of those wet things off. I'll find something for you to put on." She started to turn, then asked, "What's your name, honey?"

"Misty. Misty Jones," she managed to choke out between quiet sobs.

She wrestled with her wet shoes and socks, finally managing to peel them off. She unrolled the elastic bandage. Her ankle was huge and blotchy purple.

The "something" Anna found for her to put on proved to be men's woolen socks, and a pair of Anna's jeans, which Misty slipped on without unzipping. A man-sized long-sleeved plaid shirt completed her outfit.

"Here's a belt, honey, to hold those pants up."

"I can't tell you how grateful I am, Anna."

"We'd expect the same from you if the situation was reversed. I'm just glad we were camping here and could be of help. We thought about leaving today because of the weather, but the dredging was good, so we stayed." She stopped for a breath. "Now I'm going to fix you something to eat."

Misty's stomach protested at the mention of food. "Thanks, but I don't think I could eat anything until I know Gene's safe."

"Gene as in a fellow?"

"Yes."

"Your fellow?"

My fellow. She liked the sound of that. "Yes."

"Well, now, he'd want you to keep up your strength."

Just like my mother, Misty thought lovingly. Food will fix anything. She was soon presented with beans, fried chicken, rolls, and coffee. She nibbled at the food and gulped the coffee.

Within less than an hour of Misty's arrival, two four-wheel drive vehicles rolled into camp. Four men emerged, two sheriff's deputies and two paramedics. After questioning Misty, they called for backup. Carrying a stretcher, the four took off. Watching them go, Misty trembled with a mixture of relief and anxiety.

At Anna's urging, and knowing she should keep her leg up, Misty laid down, her leg elevated on a folded blanket. The ankle ached, precluding sleep, but she didn't care. She didn't want to go to sleep until she knew Gene was safe.

Where is Sam? If he had followed her, he would have been here by now. Perhaps he did track her and arrived here, but saw Michael and Matthew, poised with rifles at the ready. *Maybe he's out there now…watching and waiting for a chance to attack.* She shuddered.

The aching in Misty's ankle subsided. In spite of herself, she dozed, entering and leaving a twilight zone of sleep. Like bees buzzing in her ears, she heard her rescuers speak, but she couldn't understand what they said. She heard another vehicle arrive. More voices.

Drifting into a deeper sleep, Misty was abruptly awakened by Anna's voice. "Here they come!"

She leapt up from her pallet and hobbled out of the tent. Anna and her sons had flashlight shining on the trail, guiding the way for the bedraggled line of men.

Where is Gene? Misty wanted to shout. She couldn't see anyone on a stretcher. Sam, hands cuffed behind his back, walked beside a sheriff's deputy.

At last, she saw Gene. Walking! In her stocking feet, she semi-skipped toward him.

It took Gene a moment to realize that the baggy moppet heading toward him was Misty. He braced himself for a direct hit. Then his arms were around her. He wanted to lift her and swing her, but his injured leg wouldn't allow such punishment.

A soft sob escaped from her throat.

"Hey," he said, "everything's fine. It's over. We're both safe."

She pulled away from him. "What do you mean by walking?" she asked accusingly. "You said you couldn't walk."

"Fred here–" he gestured to one of the paramedics "– fixed me up."

Unconvinced, she said, "You lied to me. You could have walked! You just said that you couldn't to get rid of me."

"Well, you couldn't walk fast because of your ankle and I would've been slowed down with my leg and Sam would have caught up with us. I couldn't take that chance."

She took a step back. "I'm beginning to see the picture. You didn't stay hidden like you promised you would."

"I didn't promise."

"You did something macho–something that could have gotten you killed."

He grinned. "It worked, too"

Momentarily, she closed her eyes, then swallowed the fear of what could have happened to him. "What did you do?" she asked, not sure she wanted to know.

"The old rock trick," he answered. "Sam's not too bright, you know. I threw a rock and when he turned to the sound I tackled him. I trussed him up with my belt and waited."

Briefly, Misty empathized with Gene when he learned that she had slid down the mountain. "So you were having yourself a fine old time while I was painfully trudging along, seeking help, worried sick."

"That's a slight overstatement. I wasn't exactly comfortable or without worry myself."

They stared at each other, their gazes softening.

"Hey," one of the deputies called. "How about socializing another time? We've got to get going."

The deputies took charge of their prisoner while Gene and Misty were directed to ride with the paramedics to the nearest hospital in the foothill town of Auburn.

In the back seat, Gene wrapped a comforting arm around Misty's shoulder. She scooted closer, resting her head on his shoulder.

"I like your outfit," Gene said. "You look like Dopey."

"I tried for Snow White, but this is the best I could

do."

"Dopey was always my favorite."

She turned her head to look at him. "Did Sam tell you what he was up to?"

"Wouldn't say a thing. Not a word."

"Maybe the police will get him to talk."

Relaxed and content in Gene's embrace, Misty felt a pang of disappointment when the hospital came into view. *What would tomorrow bring? What about all the other tomorrows? I can't think of life without him.*

The rescue vehicle pulled up to the emergency entrance. Both paramedics hopped out, secured wheelchairs and pushed Gene and Misty into the hospital.

In the emergency room they were ushered into separate cubicles. A yawning physician examined Misty's ankle and ordered X-rays. No fractures.

"But you've done considerable damage to the ankle's supporting structures by walking on it," the doctor explained. "You're to rest it and elevate it–that means above the level of your heart. No walking. We'll fit you with some crutches." He demonstrated to Misty how she was to apply the elastic support bandage. "You can take it off at night," he said, "but put it on in the morning before you get out of bed."

"How about driving?" she asked hopefully.

"No driving. Check with your own doctor in a couple of days."

She sighed. "And how about Gene Haynes?"

"He seems to be in good condition. It was a flesh wound, but he'll be admitted overnight for observation.

We're putting him on antibiotics to prevent infection."

A nurse entered the cubicle. "A policeman would like to question Ms. Jones," she said.

"Okay, let him in."

The doctor and nurse left and a uniformed police officer entered.

Her mind occupied with thoughts of Gene, Misty struggled to answer the officer's questions accurately. When he was finished, the officer asked her if she had a way home.

"Yes...I'll call my roommate to pick me up."

An orderly wheeled Misty to the nearest telephone. She dialed her home number. When the recorder answered, she hung up. On impulse, she dialed Raymond's number. He answered.

"Sorry to disturb you, Raymond, but is Lorna there?"

"Uh, why yes. We were just watching a video."

I'm not her mother, Misty wanted to respond, but she said, "I need to speak with her."

"I'm sure she'd like to speak with you, too. Your disappearance has caused her a great deal of distress." His disapproving tone rankled her.

"Misty," Lorna exclaimed. "Where have you been? I've been so worried! I called everybody but your parents. I was going to contact the police in the morning."

Lorna's concern warmed Misty, but caused guilt feelings at the same time. She hadn't thought of Lorna at all over the past two days. Between her roommate's gasps of horror, Misty synopsized the events that had been keeping her occupied. "I know it's a terrible imposition, but could you come pick me up?"

"Well, my goodness, what are friends for? Of course I'll come pick you up. I'll leave right now."

"Don't rush, now. Drive safely."

Knowing it would take Lorna the better part of an hour to arrive, Misty wheeled herself back to the emergency room and told the nurse she wanted to see Gene.

The nurse picked up the telephone receiver, pushed a few buttons, and had a short conversation. Cradling the receiver, she said to Misty, "He's in a room by himself, so it's okay. But just a few minutes."

"Yes," Misty agreed. "Just a few minutes."

The orderly wheeled her to Gene's room. Two policemen were just leaving.

"I'll pick you up in five minutes," the orderly said, then disappeared.

Gene sat in a semi-reclining position, his injured leg elevated. A two-day growth of burnt orange whiskers colored his face. He looked wonderful. Suddenly, she felt tacky. Why hadn't she looked in a mirror before coming up here? With her Dopey clothes and chaotic hair, she must look like a homeless bag lady.

"How's the ankle?" he asked, his eyelids at half-staff.

How tired he must be. At least she had gotten a little sleep in her rescuers' tent. "It's just a sprain. I have to stay off it."

"Crutches?" he asked.

"Yes." She felt tongue tied, not knowing what to say to this man she loved. They had been so tender, so close the night before. Even on the ride to the hospital they reveled in their nearness. But their adventure was over and now the few feet that separated them might as well be a vast chasm. "I can't drive for a while," she added.

"Looks like we'll both be laid up for a time," he said, staring at his bandaged leg.

"Your beard is redder than your other hair," she blurted out, then flushed at the personal remark.

He glanced at her and grinned. "Does it match your face?"

She laughed nervously, then regained control of herself. "No, I'm sure my face is a pale red, but your beard has more of an orange tint."

They gazed wordlessly, longingly at each other.

The orderly reappeared. "I have to get back to emergency," he said. He grasped the handles of the wheelchair.

"Of course," Misty said. "Thanks for bringing me up."

"How are you getting home?" Gene asked.

"Lorna will be here soon."

He nodded. "Have a safe trip."

The orderly turned the wheelchair around; Misty was grateful for that so Gene couldn't see the tears filling her eyes.

While waiting in the emergency room, she was given a demonstration of crutch walking. Lorna and Raymond soon arrived, ready to whisk her home. She sat in the back of Raymond's car, right leg elevated on the seat. Between her friends' questions, she dozed.

Once home, Misty removed her elastic bandage, soaked in the bathtub, then climbed wearily into bed. In a dream-like state, she pictured herself eating a poisoned apple, falling into a trance, then being awakened by Gene's kiss...

Chapter 12

The telephone jangled on Gene's bedside table.

"Hi. It's Misty. How was your night?"

"Noisy as hell," he responded. "They must have been having a party at the nurses' station. I can't wait to get out of here."

"Has the doctor released you?"

"Yeah. He just left. I was about to call Dave to–"

"No," she interrupted. "That won't be necessary. Lorna and Raymond are getting a ride up to Gold Run to pick up our cars. They'll stop by the hospital on the way to give you some clean clothes and collect your car key. Then they'll stop again to pick you up on their way back."

Just like her to take charge, Gene thought irritably.

"Raymond?" he repeated incredulously. "I don't want that guy touching my car."

"Now be nice. He's trying to make up for being an ass and it wouldn't hurt if you did the same. You did humiliate him, you know."

Gene growled into the receiver.

"They'll be there shortly, so smile, and look

221

appreciative."

"Right." He dropped the receiver in its cradle.

Lorna breezed in a short while later and plopped a bundle of clothing on his bed. Raymond had enough sense to stay in the car, Gene mused.

"Hope these are all right," Lorna said. "And I hope you don't mind my rummaging through your things. Misty gave me your key."

"They'll do fine, Lorna. Appreciate it." He passed her his car keys.

"See you later. Toodle-do." Like a brief storm, she was gone.

With a nursing assistant hovering nearby, Gene crutch-walked to the bathroom, then insisted on privacy while he took a tub bath, his bandaged right leg dangling over the side. Shaving made him feel almost human again

Dressing proved to be a problem. He couldn't get his accessorized right leg into his jeans. With a razor blade, he slit the right outside seam of his pants.

A nurse appeared with a wheelchair. "Your carriage, sir," she said, smiling.

"Huh?"

"Your friend is downstairs in the lobby waiting to take you home."

He eyed the wheelchair. "I can use the crutches just fine. I don't need to ride in that thing."

"Hospital policy. Have a seat."

Cursed with bossy females today, Gene grumbled silently. Reluctantly, he sat and submitted to being wheeled to the lobby.

Good god. Raymond was in the lobby. Now why was he here instead of Lorna?

"What happened to Lorna?" Gene asked.

"No words of greeting?" Raymond responded.

Gene's eyes narrowed. "Just because Misty and Lorna roped you into this doesn't mean we have to pretend to be old friends."

Raymond tilted his head in a gesture of disdain. "But we could be civil."

"Sure. Hi, Ray. How the hell have you been?"

Raymond arched one brow and made a clicking sound with his tongue. "To answer your original question, Lorna insisted on rushing home to see to Misty's needs."

"Okay, so we're stuck with each other. Let's get going."

The nurse wheeled Gene outside to the car and transferred him in the front seat.

A difficult silence reigned while Raymond eased the car into the freeway traffic. Raymond finally announced, "I dropped the idea of a lawsuit."

"Big of you."

Heavy silence.

Raymond again broke it with, "Misty says you saved her life."

"She saved her own life. Maybe mine, too."

"Modesty becomes you."

"You ought to try it once in a while."

Raymond harrumphed. "Do you want to stop by to

see Misty before going to what you euphemistically call 'home'?"

Gene hesitated, warring with himself. "No, I don't think so."

Raymond nodded. "I see."

"And just what the hell do you think you see?"

"That all is not well between you two."

Gene felt his temperature rising. "Unless you want to get clobbered with a crutch, leave Misty out of this."

"As you wish." He paused. "However, Lorna is concerned about Misty's emotional state."

"She had a bad couple of days and her ankle hurts. She'll get over it." *But will I?*

Raymond *tsked*. "Even you couldn't be that dense." He exited the freeway at Sixteenth Street, maneuvered the car past Capitol Park, and finally pulled up in front of the deli. He cut the engine.

Gene was surprised to hear Raymond heave a deep sigh.

"Perhaps," Raymond said, "we share similar dilemmas."

"I don't have a dilemma," Gene protested. He turned to look at Raymond's profile. The man's dark brows were lowered, eyes staring straight ahead, and he was gnawing on his lower lip. White knuckled, he clutched the steering wheel as if trying to steady himself.

Gene had been so self-absorbed that he hadn't noticed the obvious emotional distress Raymond was suffering. A guy in that much torment couldn't be all bad, he concluded.

"How about a beer?" Gene offered.

Scowling, Raymond turned to face Gene. His brows returned to their normal position. "I believe I'd like that," he said.

Misty's phone rang.

"Hullo."

"How's the ankle?"

The sound of Gene's voice blended into a mixture of relief and rage in her belly. She hadn't spoken to him for three days, not since she called him at the hospital. She had determined not to call him again. She knew he owed her a call–at least for a word of thanks for arranging to get him and his car back to Sacramento.

"The doctor said I could start putting weight on it. How's your leg?"

"Doing well. I heard from the police this morning."

"And?"

"And it seems our friend Sam has a string of aliases. He's been involved in a number of scams. He was trying to go straight when he worked for me and went to truck driving school, but the temptation to sell tainted seafood that was supposed to be discarded was just too great. He had been selling it in small batches, but he got greedy."

"And thank goodness he got caught."

"Right. He was after us because he didn't want to go to jail again. Seems he'd already served two stretches."

"I suppose we'll have to testify in court."

"Suppose so."

An awkward silence followed.

Misty inhaled deeply, striving to quell the storm within. "Well, thanks for calling. I'd been wondering about Sam."

Gene cleared his throat. "I've been meaning to call to, uh, thank you, and Lorna for getting me and my car home."

A bit belated, she groused silently. "Raymond had a hand in it, too."

"Uh-huh. Raymond and I decided to call a truce."

"That's nice."

"Well, I'll talk to you later."

"Sure. Bye."

She wondered if that would be the last time she'd hear from him. Probably so. She thought she'd prepared for the emptiness she expected to feel when their relationship ended, but it was like being prepared for a fire. Salvage what you can, but the loss is great.

Lorna bounced into Misty's bedroom. "Here's the newspaper." She tossed it to her roommate.

"Thanks." Perusing the want ads and making phone inquiries about jobs would keep her occupied for a while.

"Was that Gene you were talking to?"

"Yes."

Smiling, Lorna tapped her foot and shook her head impatiently. "Well?"

"He and Raymond no longer despise each other."

"Yes, isn't that nice? Raymond even went to visit Gene yesterday."

Surprised, Misty glanced up sharply. "He did?"

"Uh-huh. He said Gene's working in the deli already,

getting set to re-open."

Not wanting to pursue that topic of conversation, Misty opened the newspaper and pretended to be absorbed in the want ads. When Lorna left the room, Misty put the newspaper down. She was suddenly numb, unfeeling. She managed to robot her way through the day as well as the next few days and, because she was resigned to not hearing from Gene ever again, felt ambivalent when he called. His voice both warmed her and brought back pain and anguish.

"How's the ankle?" he asked.

"Better every day." *I wish my heart were.* "I've done away with the crutches and just use an elastic bandage."

"Great. My crutches are gone, too." He paused. "Uh...I'm planning a grand re-opening."

"Oh. When?"

"Tomorrow. Haven't done any advertising, so I don't expect a big crowd. But I thought, well, if you haven't found a job yet...have you?"

"I have a couple of interviews lined up."

"Hope they work out for you. But, uh, if you and your ankle are willing and able, could you come help me out until you find something else?" Then he quickly added, "Tomorrow won't be hard on your ankle. Should be an easy day."

Jumbled thoughts raced through Misty's head. She could use the money. But was money just an excuse to see Gene again? On the other hand, she had to go back to retrieve her dried arrangements, she reasoned.

"Misty?" he inquired anxiously.

"I'm still here. Just thinking. I'll need to be off when my interviews are scheduled."

"No problem."

"Okay then, but just until I get another job."

"Understood. And hopefully by then I'll have another waitress."

"Server."

"Yeah, server." She heard him take a ragged breath. "One other thing."

"Yes?"

"I've had a lot of time to think these past few days."

So have I, Misty mused, and they haven't been comforting thoughts.

"To sort things out, and bounce ideas off a...a friend," he continued. "And I've reached a conclusion."

Good for you, she thought sarcastically. "Which is?"

"I know my color vision problem is genetic, but maybe every trait that runs in a family isn't necessarily inherited." He paused. "That is, just because a trait runs in a family, that doesn't mean every member of that family will have the same trait. Specifically, I mean just because several people in a family have had bad marriages doesn't necessarily mean than everyone in the family will."

She held her breath, not daring to hope what this remarkable conclusion was leading to.

"And," he continued, "If someone wants something, like a relationship–"

"A permanent relationship?"

"Yes, like a lasting marriage relationship badly

enough...well, regardless of the person's family background, the person could work really hard at maintaining and even improving that relationship. Do you agree?"

Misty swallowed hard, picturing Gene's face tensing with the effort to continue in this vein. "Relationships are always evolving," she responded. "A person needs to be sure to marry someone who is just as willing to work hard at the relationship, to be certain the paths the parties involved travel are parallel and not divergent."

"Excellent point. Do you think if each person in such a marriage has their own business instead of working together in one business that this would be parallel or divergent?"

"*Hmm*. It could be either. But perhaps they could consider merging their interests into a single business partnership."

"Uh—one party has considered that deeply, but the other party is insistent on owning her own business."

Misty felt her heart pick up speed. "Perhaps she hadn't considered the possibility of a partnership with him. Perhaps, if she looked at the situation from all angles, she would feel that a business partnership with one she loved would be just as satisfying to her as owning her own business. Perhaps even more satisfying."

"Excellent. And if this pair had already worked together in reasonable harmony, don't you suppose they could make a go of a permanent partnership?"

Misty gulped a ragged breath. "I think it's likely."

"Even though the girl—er, woman, wants to be

independent?"

"I've been considering that a permanent romantic entanglement, that is, marriage, does not necessarily preclude self-sufficiency and a strong degree of independence."

"I couldn't agree more. I never cared for leeches or clinging vines."

Misty wasn't successful in stifling a giggle. "On the other hand, it's okay for people to need each other."

"Absolutely," he agreed. "And to be inter-dependent."

"Another point is, I think an important aspect of any permanent relationship is mutual trust."

"Yes. Trust is of major importance," he agreed.

"For instance, if one party needs assistance in discerning colors, he should have enough trust in the empathy of the other party to ask for help, knowing full well he will not be ridiculed or be made a laughingstock."

He hesitated. "Exactly. Whatever assistance one party needs, he or she should feel comfortable asking the other person."

She gave a hearty laugh. It felt wonderful. She couldn't remember the last time she had even chuckled.

When she quieted, he said, "So maybe you don't need to keep those appointments for interviews?"

"No, perhaps not."

"Good. And let's work out the details of this partnership tomorrow."

Tomorrow? She was aghast. What's wrong with right now, she wanted to shriek. Why don't you rush over here and kiss me till I'm giddy? Or I'd be more than willing to rush over there. And never leave. She sighed.

She managed to grind out a "Right. Tomorrow." She clicked off her cell phone.

In a quandary, Misty sank down on her bed. In her mind, she replayed the tape of their conversation. Did she misinterpret what he had said, she wondered. Did he propose marriage? If so, it was the strangest proposal she'd ever heard of. He never mentioned love. Did he love her? Does he care whether or not she loves him? Apparently, that's not important to him. A business partnership. That's what he's after. He knows she's a good worker and a smart businesswoman. He doesn't want her seeking another job, he wants her at his deli so he can concentrate his efforts on food preparation and leave the business details to her. And, of course, she'd be a convenient bed partner. The heel.

On the other hand, they had talked about trust. Maybe she wasn't trusting. She'd have to see what the next day would bring.

The mighty engine of the fishing boat shuddered, reluctant to awaken, then snarled to life. Dawn was an hour away, but the two fisherman moved about the craft performing their well-rehearsed myriad duties.

Gene's concentration was broken by Misty's arrival. He looked up from the murky icing ocean he'd created to luxuriate in her presence. Her complexion glowed and her hair shimmered, sleek and shining. *My wife*. She's going to be my wife. The blissful thought gladdened and warmed him. Before they had spoken on the telephone the night before, his gut had been an ocean of curling, swelling waves. But when she agreed to marry him, he became a calm, placid contented lake.

She smiled at him, but the smile appeared tentative and her hooded eyes had a vacant quality. She certainly didn't appear to be a woman who'd just received and accepted a marriage proposal. He wanted to go to her, to take her in his arms, but his apron was tossed with a mixture of various salads and his hands were covered with the gray icing he was using to depict fog.

"Hi," he called out.

"Hi. Oh! You're doing a cake. May I see it?"

"Sure."

Her smile broadened and her eyes regained their normal sparkle. He must have imagined her discontent, he concluded. She fairly skipped to his side to see his latest work of art. He leaned over and kissed her on the cheek. "It's good to see you," he said. "Better than good." He wanted her to turn her lips to him, but she just looked at the cake.

"A fishing boat," she said without enthusiasm.

She sounded disappointed. Why would she be disappointed? Probably too gray. "Not very colorful, I'm afraid."

"It's perfect for the setting. Early morning. Wet and eerie. The fishermen are anxious to be off, hoping for a good day's catch."

Pleased, he said, "That's just the spirit I was trying to capture." But her tone wasn't right, her affect was flat.

"Who's it for?" she asked.

"A couple of buddies who just bought a commercial fishing boat. Dave wants to have a little celebration for them tonight."

"Oh." She turned, picked up the salt and pepper containers, and went to the tables to refill the shakers. He noted her plodding steps. Usually, her feet skimmed across the floor.

What was wrong, he wondered. When he had talked to her on the telephone the day before, she was actually laughing. He had expected her to rush into the deli this morning bubbling with delight and cover him with passionate kisses.

He quickly finished the cake and boxed it. He removed his soiled apron and cleaned himself up. Hands full of salt and pepper, Misty had her back to Gene. He went to her and started to circle her with is arms, but damn! Their first customer arrived.

Business was slow but steady, so he didn't have a chance to talk with her until the last customer left and he began preparing lunch for the two of them.

"No gourmet lunch today, I'm afraid," he said. "Just turkey and Swiss on sour dough."

Seemingly occupied with wiping tables, she didn't respond.

She's having second thoughts, he concluded. She doesn't want to marry me after all. His gut spasmed. Determined to make a go of their relationship, he wasn't going to give up without a fight. He went to her, grasped both of her shoulders, turned her to face him, and said,

"Misty, honey, what's the matter?"

Slowly, she looked up and silently met his gaze.

"I wish I could read your mind, sweetheart," he said, "but I can't. You have to tell me what's wrong."

Her lips thinned and the corners of her mouth down turned. "Did you propose marriage or simply a business partnership yesterday? If it was marriage, it was the weirdest, most unromantic proposal I've ever heard of."

Weird? Unromantic? Actually, he'd thought it was pretty clever. And, of course, unique. What did she want him to do–drop down on one knee? He'd always considered her too sensible and down-to-earth for that.

She wiggled her shoulders out of his grasp. "I have to go home," she said, her voice breaking. She turned on her heel and fled out the door.

Dumfounded, Gene raised a hand in protest and started to call her, but thought better of it.

He cut the sandwiches in half and ate them both. Damn. If she didn't quit storming out on him, he'd weigh three hundred pounds.

"I'm never going back to the deli," Misty muttered as she entered her apartment. She sniffed long and hard and brushed tears of sadness and rage off her cheeks. He'll just have to arrange for a new business partnership. Maybe his next server will be strictly cerebral.

Trust. Ha! Even when I clearly told him how I felt about his idiotic proposal he just looked at me as if I were an extinct creature from Jurassic Park. He has no concept of a woman's needs and desires. He knows only himself. Women exist solely for his needs, his pleasures.

Even as Misty hurled these silent insults at Gene, she had momentary flashes of recognition that they might not be entirely deserved. Yet, she continued to fuel her anger because it helped to mask her pain.

She went to the refrigerator and poured a glass of milk. Then she changed into shorts and decided to work on the carpets. She was occupied in vigorously vacuuming when Lorna breezed in.

"My goodness, what are you doing?" Lorna asked. "I just vacuumed the whole place yesterday. Don't you remember?"

"Guess I forgot." She stopped vacuuming.

Lorna shook her head in bewilderment then disappeared into her room. Soon, Misty heard her roommate singing in the shower.

Misty put the vacuum cleaner away, then wandered aimlessly around the apartment. Eventually, she reached her own bathroom, filled the tub with water as hot as she could tolerate and soaked until her skin puckered. She dressed in lounging pajamas, returned to the living room, sank onto the couch, and picked up a *Ladies' Home Journal*. She read the first paragraph of "Can This Marriage Be Saved?" three times without understanding a word. Disgusted, she dropped the magazine on the coffee table. It didn't help that Lorna, now out of the shower, was skimming around her room, singing. Off key.

Lorna emerged from her room wearing a new dinner dress. A silk mauve creation, it whispered against her breasts and hips, and accentuated her slender waist. She wore a diamond pendant and matching drop earrings. She moved directly in front of Misty, struck a model's pose, and twirled.

"Wow," Misty exclaimed. "You're beautiful. All this loveliness just for Raymond?"

Lorna's cheeks pinked prettily.

"Did you go into hock for the diamonds?"

Lorna averted her gaze and didn't answer.

Misty sat up straight. "Raymond gave them to you, didn't he?"

"Well, yes."

Their buzzer rang. Lorna glided to the door to admit Raymond. The pair gazed at each other with such love that Misty thought her heart would shatter with longing.

Raymond took Lorna's hand and tucked it in the crook of his elbow. "Did you tell her?" he asked.

She lowered her eyes. "Of course not, dear. You asked me not to."

As if that would stop you, Misty thought.

He kissed the top of Lorna's head. "I think it's time to tell, Snookums. Don't you?"

"If you say so, Sweetums."

Misty felt as though she had just swallowed a gallon of syrup. She wished they'd make their big announcement and get it over with.

"Misty," Raymond began, "we want you to be the first to know that Lorna and I have made an eternal commitment to one another. This evening we're celebrating our engagement."

Misty swallowed her tears and tried to look surprised.

Dinner for Two

With a mingling of happiness for them and sorrow for herself, she jumped up from the couch to hug them both. "I hope you'll always be as happy as you are now."

The pair's attention returned to each other. Misty wistfully watched as they floated out the door.

Alone. Misty had never felt so alone. She was quite certain that at that moment in time there was no one else in the entire universe quite as alone as she was.

She tried switching on the television, but Gene's face replaced the newscaster's, his rugged features fading in and out.

No doubt he's enjoying himself at that raucous party for the fishermen, she thought. She pictured a room full of boisterous, beer drinking, back slapping men. Then she tensed at the thought of lovely, long-legged women mingling with the men, just like in the beer commercials. And all the women would make a ridiculous fuss over Gene's cake.

She recalled her excitement when she'd entered the deli that morning and realized Gene was doing a cake. She was so sure it was for her–for them. Depicting an ethereal, romantic scene, probably of the Elizabethan era– a man and woman gazing at each other, perhaps him slipping a ring on her finger. She relived the stinging disappointment she felt at seeing a fishing boat. Her heart ached. Her whole body ached.

The buzzer rang.

She didn't respond. She couldn't face anyone this evening.

It rang again. A voice called out, "*Dinner for Two*!"

Stunned, she slowly rose, then flew to the door and fumbled with the knob before managing to yank it open. Gene stood before her, his arms full of supplies. Surely he was the handsomest of men.

He smiled, but glanced at her only briefly before walking past her into the kitchen.

"I hope you like Steak Diane," he said.

Incredulous, she stood still as a statue, only her eyes in motion, following his movements.

He returned to her, closed the door, and with his index finger lifted her chin until she had eye contact with him. He bowed his head to kiss her lightly on the lips. He slipped an arm around her shoulders. "Come into the living room." He guided her in and gently directed her to sit on the couch.

With wide eyes, Misty silently watched as Gene placed a champagne bucket near her, then unfolded the small round table. He covered it with a cream-colored cloth and used his finest China, silver, and crystal to set the table. She gulped when he placed Cupid candleholders on the center of the cloth. She ordered her eyes not to leak.

Next, Gene carried a cake box into the living room. Misty knew it wouldn't depict a fishing scene. Would it be as lovely as the cake he had created for Dave and Julie?

"I'd like to show you our desert," he said.

Carefully, he lifted the small rectangular cake out of its box and proudly displayed it to Misty. Shocked at the first sight of it, she blinked and looked again. The cake was decorated with a pair of frogs. A long-lashed female frog, gowned in sheer, flowing chiffon, stood next to a Kermit-styled, bow-tied male frog that, on bended knee, had his hands crossed over his heart. The inscription read, "Marry me or I'll croak."

Misty's tentative giggle led to a gale of laughter. Gene smiled, pleased with her reaction.

If this is his intrinsic idea of romance, she thought, so be it. She could live with that.

Gene twirled a bottle of champagne in its bucket then popped the cork. He poured the bubbly, fizzing liquid and offered her a glass. He sat on the couch next to her. Wordlessly they clinked their glasses together and sipped.

Something in the bottom of her glass caught Misty's eyes. She held the glass up to the light. A diamond ring sparkled back at her. Now *that* was romantic!

Like a volcano, Misty exploded. She flung her arms around Gene's neck and planted her lips on his, throwing him off balance. He righted himself and set both glasses of champagne on the coffee table. Then his arms were around her and his hungry lips devoured hers.

As one, they stood and edged toward her bedroom.

Later, when the steak was room temperature and the bubbles had drowned in the neglected champagne, Misty snuggled closer to Gene, brushing her hand over the downy, russet hair on his chest. "Darling, there's something you should know."

"*Hmm.* Let me guess. You love me almost as much as I love you."

"I love you more," she said. "But that's not it."

"You have the most sensuous lips among all Homo Sapiens."

"No. That honor goes to you. Try again."

He kissed the tip of her nose, then nibbled at her earlobe. "That you use the most expensive perfumes available to create your fresh, lemon scent."

"No...but speaking of scent–" she pressed her nose against his neck and inhaled deeply "–you always smell of delicious, gourmet foods. Care to try again?"

"You're going to leave me because a Hollywood agent wants to recruit you for your sultry, come-hither voice."

She made a deep, throaty sound. "Close," she teased, "but what I have to tell you is really more of a confession...."

His interest piqued, he said, "Go on. And whatever it is, I'll love you anyway."

"Well, we both know I promised I would be trustworthy and never laugh or ridicule, but–"

He groaned. "Oh, no."

"Yes, dear. Frogs are not maroon."

The End

Meet the Author:

Although writer-editor Arlene Evans has written and published short stories and numerous articles, this is her debut novel. Living in the Sierra-Nevada, her favorite outdoor activity is hiking the area's many trails. While working as a school nurse, she discovered how common colorblindness is and the challenges people face because of it. When she could find no literature for children or teens on the disorder, she wrote two non-fiction books, one for children and one for teens through adults. Her website is: www.CVDbooks.com. The hero of *Dinner for Two,* Gene Haynes, is colorblind, which poses several challenges for him.

Also available from Echelon Press Publishing

While the Daffodils Danced (Women's Fiction)
Cathi LaMarche

Pregnant by a married man, Cara faces the devastation of offering her child up for adoption. Having made the ultimate sacrifice, she seeks solace in her field of daffodils. But in the shadow of her pain, Cara finds a kindred spirit, forging an unbreakable friendship that sustains her through lost love and the betrayal by those she loves the most.

$15.99   ISBN 1-59080-402-3

Justice Incarnate (Women's Adventure)
Regan Black

Whoever said, "you only live once" didn't know Jaden Michaels. Attacked by an evil nobleman in 1066, her life took a dramatic detour. In the following millennium, she's lived repeatedly with one goal: eliminate the demon that preys on women and children. Now, in 2096, Jaden must fight to find the one weapon that will banish him forever.

$13.99   ISBN 1-59080-386-8

Laura's Secret (Romantic Suspense)
Shannon Greenland

Mysterious Laura Genny knows how to hide her dark past. Always wary and on the move, she accepts a lifelong dream position as a sound engineer with an international rock group. But when lead guitarist Will Burns gets too close, she must decide if love is worth the price of exposure.

$13.99   ISBN 1-59080-415-5

Operation: Stiletto (Romantic Suspense)
T.A. Ridgell

Teamed with Python, an ex-wrestler struggling to slay a multitude of inner demons, Special Agent Kendal Smart will do anything to infiltrate the wrestling culture and eradicate a deadly crime ring. Even if it means wearing skintight clothes, stilettos, and immersing herself in a bizarre, sexually overt world.

$14.49   ISBN 1-59080-393-0

Also available from Echelon Press Publishing

Three Strikes You're Dead (Golden Age Mystery)
Robert Goldsborough

In the mob-ridden Chicago of 1938, a reform candidate for mayor is gunned down, and Steve Malek, a police reporter for *The Tribune*, senses the story of a lifetime. Incurring his editors' anger, he ranges far beyond his beat, plunging headlong into a maverick investigation of the murder.

$12.99   ISBN 1-59080-420-0

Fear of the Unknown (Horror Anthology)
Poppy Z. Brite, Jack Ketchum, Owl Goingback, *et al*

A chill wind blows through the thirteen stories in this new collection. It rustles dead cornfields and diseased grapevines, travels through dark train tunnels and small railside towns, brushes across the killing floor of an abandoned LA shop and tugs at the garments of the bouncer at Death's own nightclub. Proceeds benefit Bone Cancer International, Inc.

$12.99   ISBN 1-59080-386-8

Pedestals (Suspense)
Jane Shoup

The last year has been a nightmare for Jack Wilmont. So when a serial killer–after a year of nothing–strikes on the first day of Jack's personal leave, he knows the nightmare is only beginning. Jack agrees to look at the evidence, but his one good deed leads him into the case of a missing nine-year-old girl abducted from her home.

$14.99   ISBN 1-59080-426-0

Redemption (Western)
Morgan J. Blake

Kinson women aren't known for sitting idly by while others decide their fates. This keeps Wylie Kinson going when his mother and sister are kidnapped in an Apache raid. But Wylie's hopes are dashed when he stands over his mother's mutilated body. Worse, he suspects the Apaches aren't responsible. If not Apaches, who would do such unspeakable acts? Vowing revenge, Wylie unravels the treacherous trail.

$15.49   ISBN 1-59080-380-9

Also available from Echelon Press Publishing

Crossing the Meadow (Horror/Ghost)
Kfir Luzzatto

A strange nightmare, a young woman in a foggy city and a body buried underneath a bathtub, all converge to force an ordinary man to investigate a dark, long forgotten past. A little girl who can see her dead cat, an old blind woman and a beautiful girl who died too young, unknowingly play a role in a game in which humanity must survive the death of the flesh.

$11.99   ISBN 1-59080-283-7

The Rosary Bride (Cozy Mystery)
Luisa Buehler

In the 1940's, the women of Regina College insisted a young woman in a 'fancy dress' haunted the halls near the chapel. Fifty years later, during the renovation of the library, workers expose a skeleton. Grace Marsden, present at the discovery is drawn into the search for the victim's identity, fearing the remains will lead to skeletons in her own family closet

$11.99   ISBN 1-59080-227-6

Why God Has Gray Hair (Humorous Memoir)
Sophia Zufa

Those were the days! Pre Vatican II, Sister Hedwig, and Father Thaddeus. Step back in time to the elementary days of the 1930's in parochial school. Zufa offers an insightful, and more times than not, humorous retelling of her youthful days. Meet neighbors, friends, and family, in the sharp-witted and emotionally inspiring collection of tales born of experience.

$10.99   ISBN 1-59080-146-6

Unbinding the Stone (Science Fiction/Fantasy)
Marc Vun Kannon

Young Tarkas, a Singer of humble roots, whose worst crime had been accidentally stumbling upon a village elder and his wife..um...in the act, suddenly finds himself exiled from the only home he's ever known. Because of a flame in the bowl. What Tarkas soon learns is that his misfortune is necessary to the future of the universe as he knows it. For he has been chosen as a Hero-in-training, and he must save the world.

$14.99   ISBN 1-59080-140-7

Printed in the United States
49198LVS00001B/36